I0525142

GIFTED: THE INTRODUCTION OF MASON SHRINEWALD

YEAR ONE

REGINALD JOHNSON

Copyright © 2018 by Reginald Johnson

All rights reserved.

No part of this book may be reproduced in any form or by any electronic or mechanical means, including information storage and retrieval systems, without written permission from the author, except for the use of brief quotations in a book review.

SMS Write On Publishing 3843 Union Road Cheektowaga, NY 14225
www.smswriteonpublishingllc.com

CONTENTS

1. This Will Be Good For You   1
2. Red Flags   13
3. Bedtime Stories   21
4. Contrivers Ball   35
5. Killer Instinct   43
6. Even if it kills me   49
7. What am I?   61
8. The Thirst   67
9. The Dilemma   72
10. Mason's Meeting   79
11. The Offer   85
12. Mason's First Trial   91
13. The Trial of Temptation   99
14. The Final Trial   105
15. Nebulous Opaque   112
16. Clive Mountain   117
17. Separation for the Hunt   126

THIS WILL BE GOOD FOR YOU

*T*he clouds had grown weary and began to cry. Aimlessly I attempted to count each drop as it landed onto the roof; for this would be far better than being lectured again by my parents on how I shouldn't waste my gifts. It also didn't help with each conversation my father would add "kids would die to be in your position". Would they really, I thought? This will be good for you Mason; the school has been ranked number one for over 25 years. "The school's also famous for its unique variety of students who attend." My mom said. I mainly watched their mouths move while I pondered about what I could do to evade this conversation.

My parents have always been so ambitious; I, on the other hand, haven't found anything of interest to be ambitious about. I mean sure it's true that I took the term responsibility lightly, but how they spoke about Luce, the school of the gifted seemed more like a punishment than a trek to find myself. In three days, I would be leaving home for a school I know absolutely nothing about. My parents have always been on the elusive side, but this time they had gone too far. I walked through the dark halls of our house aimlessly thinking about all the things my parents had accomplished. My father Nero Shrinewald, the middle child of six, had accomplished much in life, in such a short time period. He had finished graduate school by the time he was twenty-three, although sometimes his word choice didn't make it visible on how educated he was. Next, he went on to become one of the world's greatest chef's. The odd part about father is he never ate any of his food. Now and then father would dabble in the recording industry and release songs, but he never pursued it. Father claimed it was a gruesome business. My father, Nero Shrinewald, was a fair-skinned man with jet black hair and gray eyes. He is half black and half Hispanic. He was born in Baton Rouge, Louisiana. His facial expressions were often cold with a sinister smile that was sharp enough to cut through any tension. His build was not quite the one of a model, but not quite as large as a football player. Father's smile made you smile; he had an obsessive-compulsive condition with his teeth, they favored porcelain veneers. Father was constantly at the dentist, I found it rather hilarious. My mother, Mona Shrinewald, never looked a day over thirty-five, when in reality this October she'd be fifty-five. How mother kept herself so well put together, I'll never know. Mother grew up on the reservation in the mountains in Pennsylvania where life was simple. A place where there was never too much to do but fish, ski, hike and a myriad of other outdoor life activities. Mother didn't draw father in with her beauty although it helped. Instead, it was her big heart and relentless curiosity of life. Simple things always appeased the two; they claimed to have enough complexity in their lives, I disagreed. I don't know what other families were like, but I had a feeling deep down inside that most families weren't like mine.

My things were packed, and I sat in the shower for a few hours until I was tired enough to lay down but the feeling never came. I laid in my bed and watched the ceiling fan rotate with a glass of scotch in hand, sipping slowly. Twelve glasses in, I went to father's office to grab another bottle. I was drinking as if I had no place to be in the morning, but I didn't care. There was so much on my mind and anxiety residing within me, I'd probably never fall asleep. The sun came up, and I grew tired, and as usual, I would spend the day exhausted walking around like a zombie. My parents and I arrived at the airport around 8 am. My father, as usual, smiled and maintained his calm and collected composure. As if he knew tomorrow and each day that followed would be a sure thing. My mom looked sad with tears in her eyes and smiled, "learn all you can Mason" she told me. "I will," I replied. "Promise me you won't become a worry wart while I'm gone". She ignored my request. Instead, she repeated; "this will be good for you".

I approached security after hugging and kissing my parents and proceeded towards my gate. On the plane, I tried once more to catch some z's, but it was no use. Between the lady constantly chastising her children and the strange kid ranting to himself too low and fast for me to understand him, I knew this would be a long flight. Instead, I picked up a TIME magazine and noticed that the school I was attending this fall was on the front page. I flipped through the table of contents and found the cover page feature; once I got to the page, I noticed a picture of a woman. The woman looked possibly a few years older than I was. That would have been difficult to believe because the article stated that she had been with the school for about fifteen years. The picture of her was intense to the point where I felt as if she stared back at me. It approached 12:30 pm, and the captain announced that we had reached our destination. All I kept hearing is mother's words "this will be good for you," I hope she was right. While unloading the plane, I noticed that the airport was unlike any other I had ever seen in my life, and I've been everywhere. Classical music played throughout the airport, and it seemed as if everything and everyone moved rapidly but in slow motion. Not one person acknowledged the next as if no one needed assistance with anything. Throughout the airport, there were blood banks, and there were various forms of incentives for blood donors. Blood banks were everywhere and advertisements; some offered to absolve debt, others offered sky miles, and some simply offered you money. Why would they go through these extremes and why were they so aggressive about people donating? As I advanced toward baggage claims, I ran into the same kid who had been on the plane, he was now on the train. Again, he seemed preoccupied and muttering in the same undertone; fast and too low for me to comprehend what he was saying. For a moment he glanced up and gazed at me, he seemed troubled. The train's door opened at my stop, I got off and walked toward baggage claims. At baggage claims, there was a young lady frantic about the airline forgetting her luggage, and she too spoke in a loud undertone which I could not understand. Perhaps on this side of the world people suffered from a common speech impediment. Not watching where I was walking; I accidentally bumped into her, upon impact her eyes lit up and shifted two shades dark jade. "WATCH WHERE YOU'RE WALKING!!!" she said. "Sorry," I replied. Something gave me the feeling that this fall would prove to be an interesting one.

A driver was holding a sign with my name on it. I studied him for a moment, uncertain on whether I should tell him who I was. "You're Mason Shrinewald." He said. "What if I am sir?" I replied. "Oh I know who you are young sir, why I've served the Shrinewald clan for quite some time now. There's something unique about you though young sir; I am almost sure of it!!!" He said. "I supposed you'll be driving me to campus?" I asked. "The name is Cerival Primus." He said. "Glad to meet you, sir." [shaking his hand.] As I stepped into the car, he had Miles Davis playing. "Your father chose this car especially for you. He felt it would suit you perfectly, scotch sir?" Cerival asked. The entire situation baffled me only because my father never spoke much about anyone other than mother or family. He seldom discussed his personal or business affairs with me. When I asked about how our wealth came about he always says it's from old money. The other situation that seemed difficult to grasp was the fact that my father had provided me with a driver who would now drive me around and follow me where ever I went while being away at school. Now not only did I have to worry about discovering what kind of school my parents had enrolled me in, but I now had to be concerned with drawing too much attention in an all-black Mercedes Benz S550 Special Class. I mean, was public transportation beneath me? "So, what do you know about the school for the gifted?" Cerival asked. "Well I don't know anything; my parents thought it would be nice for me to finally find myself," I said. "Find yourself. [Laughs] What are you depressed?" "No, I don't think so, it's just that I haven't found anything I love yet. I mean there are plenty of things I thrive at, but none of them interests me." I replied. "Rest assured your gifts will surface just as you need them, this school has a knack for producing results. If Mona and Nero sent you to this school, there must be a far greater reason behind their actions. Sit tight young sir, we're almost there!" said Cerival. Cerival lets out a devious snicker and shifts into fifth gear.

When we arrived at the school, there were men dressed in suits at the gate. "Good afternoon gentlemen, I am here dropping off a first-year student." Said Cerival. "What's the name, sir?" The man asked. "Mason Shrinewald." Cerival replied. The men's eyes widened as they glanced at each other and then into the car trying to peer through the car's curtain covered windows. "Welcome to Luce sir." The man replied. "Thank you, gentlemen." Cerival said. The gates sprung open and all of a sudden it became difficult to swallow, the sky was amber red, the mood of an empty autumn. The air suddenly became cold and dreary. "Apprehensive, are we?" Cerival questioned. "Only anxious," I responded. Students walked in every direction toward their classroom buildings; too intoned with themselves to notice much of anything else around them. "Mr. Shrinewald, admissions are the dark brown building furthest to the right. Once you have your classroom schedule, you'll much like to check into your living quarters and get settled in." Cerival directed. "Thanks." I replied. "Enjoy," Cerival responded.

Once I got to the admissions building, I ran into the same abrasive girl from the airport. She didn't seem like the attitude had changed much since I saw her at the airport; only this time she was more irate. This time I could hear why she was so upset because she had been screaming to the top of her lungs. "WHY IS IT SO DIFFI-CULT FOR ME TO HAVE A SOMEWHAT GOOD DAY?! FIRST MY LUGGAGE WAS STOLEN, THEN THE EXTREMELY RUDE CAB DRIVER; NOW MY CLASSES ARE FILLED, ALL OF THEM? ISN'T THERE SOME WAY I CAN FORCE REGISTER?" She asked. "Ma'am I'm sorry, but at this point, there isn't much we can do for you." The admissions lady replied. "DOES MY PARENTS HISTORY AT THIS SCHOOL HAVE ANYTHING TO DO WITH ME NOT BEING ABLE TO GET ENROLLED IN MY CLASSES? I BET THE HEADMASTER PHALANX PUT YOU UP TO THIS; WHERE IS THAT EVIL BITCH!? I WON'T ALLOW THIS SCHOOL TO TREAT ME HOW THEY TREATED MY FAMILY MEMBERS THAT CAME HERE BEFORE ME." Said the girl. This girl became hysterical and angry to the point where her words ran together. Who would want to see to it that this girl would not be able to enroll in her classes and why? Had her family history been that awful that the school would sabotage certain people at any moment for any reason? I had thought about the vague reasons my parents had pointed out to me and convinced me why attending this school would be imperative. So far all that I knew about the school was that you had to possess gifts and talents. What talents did I remotely possess to be found fit to attend a school of such stature? I left the registration building and walked to the Knox building; this building is where most of the freshmen classes took place. The halls were long, the doors were tall, and oil lamps lit the building dimly. I walked around while thinking about the classes like martial arts, English, politics or tactics? Were they training us to be spies or something? It was 12:45pm when the loudspeaker came on.

"Attention all students; headmaster Phalanx would like to have a word with you all in the auditorium. You have ten minutes to take a seat." Said the voice over the loudspeaker. "Good afternoon students! I am headmaster Sara Phalanx, and I would like to be the first to welcome you to one of the most prestigious schools in the world. For some, your family's generations have walked these halls and have sat in the very chairs you all occupy as we speak. You may have a clear focus on why you have come here, while others have yet to discover who they are and what it is, you can truly do. Many trials will be presented to you during your stay here. Some of these tasks will appear to be impossible, but I assure you, all objectives are attainable. Our rules here at Luce Academy are simple… be loyal, be honest, be respectful. Oh, and work hard." "Right- [scoffs.] Spoken like a true hypocrite, man Lady Phalanx doesn't care. She lives to make every student's life here pure hell. It's like the Phalanx Clan are born to cause anguish. They practically are talented at hurting people. I mean, who wakes up with the intention of making someone's day hell? Never mind me and my rambling, it's been a rough two months. Regis Knight's the name, [reaches out to shake Mason's hand.] "Mason Shrinewald." I replied. "Shrinewald?" says Regis. "Yes, it is a funny name, and no I'm not Jewish." [Laughs]. I replied. "No it's not that, it's just that I'm reading about someone with the same last name in my history book. What was his first name?" Says Regis trying to recollect. Regis was the gentlemen whom I ran into at the airport. I wouldn't mind him being around because he always occupied himself with his own thoughts. It made it easier for me to be around people like that because I loathe talking about myself. "SHRINEWALD!!!!" Regis shouted. "Really, how long ago was this history book written?" I asked. "Oh, this book is pretty old; my grandfather's father used the same book. It was published a year after the school was opened. It says here Nero Shrinewald, which I presume is one of your ancestors, helped build the school?" Regis asked. "May I?" I asked [reaching for his book.] "Oh, not at all, go ahead." Says Regis. "Here it says: Nero Shrinewald was born in Baton Rouge, Louisiana in 1913. He was the middle child of Prantis Shrinewald and Elizabeth Shrinewald. Nero was well known for his many contributions to the prestigious Luce School for the Gifted. Although the following statements have not been confirmed the Shrinewald Clan was believed to be something other than human. The citizens of Baton Rouge noticed their defiance to aging. Once the rumor had spread throughout the city of Baton Rouge, the Shrinewald Clan was never heard from or seen again. The school for the gifted later erected a building to honor Nero Shrinewald's contributions, Shriners Hall. "Crazy stuff, right? I mean your family has something to do with why this school even exists. That's pretty badass if you ask me!" Regis ranted. Regis went on rambling about the book and how crazy it was that I had a distant relative who helped found this school. With my wandering mind and his prattling, I knew he wouldn't have noticed me walking off.

"You're Mason Shrinewald, right?" the girl asked. "Yes, I supposed I am." I replied. "Karen Cartright." [Shaking his hand and holding onto it.] "Pleased to make your acquaintance Ms. Cartright." I said. "Oh no, the pleasure's all mines. The professors have been in a frenzy since they've learned that a new member of the Shrinewald Clan would be attending this semester." Said Karen. "Clan, what's this Clan business?" I replied. "That's right, you were born into your family's last name correct?" Karen asked. "Yes." I replied. "We don't call them families around here, it's a bit "normal" and seeing that we all have abnormal backgrounds hence the reason we attend this school we found "clan" to be more appropriate." Said Karen. "Nice, how do you like it here?" I asked. "It has its moments where it's nice but it's mainly hell." Karen replied. "So why do you attend?" I asked. "It's what my parents decided for me, Cartright tradition. It's a load of crock I tell ya. Well Mason my class is about to begin, oh and sorry for being rude the past couple of times seeing you. Bad day, you can under-stand right?" Karen asked. "Right." I replied. "So all is forgiven?" Karen asked. "Yeah. We're good." I said. "Cool, smell ya later!" Karen replied. "Peace." I said.

RED FLAGS

a couple of days had passed, and she still lingered in my head. I could still smell her on my hands. Hell, I felt like if she had kissed me, I'd probably still taste her on my breath. What a woman she was with curves laced all over. Whatever it was, this hold she had on me, I welcomed it. It seemed as time passed the more peculiar things became. The evening only flights, monotonous language that sounded like someone spoke in tongues. The airport with no restaurants, only blood banks; now an unusual textbook that suggested that my clan had a pivotal role in the creation of this school. Things weren't adding up. I thought to call my parents, but I knew that wouldn't get me very far. They'd probably insist that I divert my attention toward my studies and getting adjusted to the school. This was no ordinary school, for if it was, why wouldn't all kids be able to attend? The clock's ticks seemed to amplify as the night progressed, but as usual, I couldn't sleep. Between my obvious insomnia issue and the turbulent storm brewing outside my window, I'd be destitute of sleep. I stared at the ceiling and pondered on a variety of solutions to help me fall asleep, but seldom did I come up with one. I had the room to myself, but it still felt like the bed beneath me was occupied by another, so that kept me on edge a bit too. I grabbed the remote and tossed it around as I contemplated on what I would wear tomorrow. I also began to ponder on what Regis had shown me earlier today in his history book. How coincidental it was that one of the school's founding fathers shared the same name as my father. Pausing for a moment, with a slight feeling of disbelief, I laughed and turned on the TV. I had to do something to get my mind off of how odd this school was. I laid back and tossed the remote, frustrated that I couldn't find anything on TV to watch to distract me. I eventually left it on MTV and forced myself to watch videos that sucked. I must have dozed for a moment because I was awakened by the remote landing on top of my head and my TV had somehow been turned off. I didn't know that the outlets were on timers, but how would the timers explain the remote I chucked across the room landing on top of my head? I didn't even care; I was much too exhausted physically and mentally from the day to try to pick apart my predicament. I just rolled over and went to bed.

In politics, professor Rigby prattled on and on about America being mistakenly considered a superpower. He went on to support his opinion by claiming that not only were we behind technologically, even more culturally. Much too often did he ramble about his personal views in class. To be an opinionated old man, professor Rigby seemed to possess a young stature physically but a blatant old spirit. Not only did he teach politics, but he also taught Introduction to Tactics as well. Professor Rigby was about 5'7", with a medium build. He wore his bifocals on the ridge of his nose and constantly smoked a pipe, but his voice was as clear as water. Professor Rigby spoke rapidly at the beginning of his sentence and always seemed to slow down his speech towards the end of his sentences. His goatee was gray and was about three inches long. He always stroked it when he posed a question in class. "Mr. Knight!" Yelled Professor Rigby. "Yes, sir?" Regis replied. "Can you explain to the class the three elements that should be maintained when under pressure?" Asked Professor Rigby. "Sure I can sir, composure, a clear mind and proactive speed," Regis responded. "Very good, Mr. Knight, outstanding, for a moment I thought you would stumble, but you didn't. Class, do you know why these three elements are essential in a confrontation? No one, alright, I'll pick someone, Mr.

Shrinewald!!!" Professor Rigby yelled. "Sir?" I replied. [Damn, professor Rigby seemed to always call on me when my mind drifted off. I thought to myself.] "Well I would assume that composure, a clear mind, and proactive speed would need to be maintained so that the most suitable alternative can be chosen in a life-threatening situation." I said. "Very good Mr. Shrinewald! Remember this class, one day you will be faced with adversity. How well you can apply this technique may dictate whether you live or die. Class dismissed." Professor Rigby said. "Mr Shrinewald." Professor Rigby yelled. "Professor Rigby?" I responded. "I'll have a word with you. I couldn't help but notice that you seemed distracted this evening." Said Professor Rigby. "Yes sir, I've just been-[cutting Mason off.] "Karen Cartright has an amazing effect on those she touches. My advice to you, try not to interact with her too much, it isn't healthy for her." Said Professor Rigby. "Yes, sir," I replied. "Have a goodnight Chap." Said Professor Rigby. "Thank you, and you do the same, wait a minute, how did you know about that? How did you know her name?" I asked. "You're not the only one with gifts, sir. Goodnight." Professor Rigby replied. This school was starting to freak me out. I placed my books into my book bag and headed towards Shriners Hall.

The trees spoke in unison as the evening breeze blew through the campus. The weather was slowly changing, and I could feel the cold draft crawl up my neck. I zipped up my jacket and put on my hood. SWOOOOOM!!!! "STOP HIM IMMEDIATE-LY!!!!!!!" Headmaster Phalanx was in a rage pointing at the black blur that blew by me. Her eyes were blushed red and her face cold and stiff as stone. Her finger pointed through the air; her manicured nails flawlessly trimmed seemed to cut through the air. Headmaster Phalanx noticed me sitting there in shock trying to make sense of what just happened. Her eyebrows raised, her hands and teeth clenched tight, with her eyes closed she slowly panned over to me with an intense look of pain on her face. "Mason your hand, it's bleeding!!!!! You need to go get that looked at before it gets worse," Said Lady Phalanx. "Headmaster Ph" This time her eyes were a deeper red and her skin grew pale white. "MASON GO!!!!!!!!!" Lady Phalanx screamed. I picked myself up and grabbed my bag and fled towards Shriners Hall as fast I could. I swiped my card, dropped my bag onto the living room floor and rushed towards the bathroom for the first aid kit. Blood ran down my hand onto my fingertips. I turned on the bathroom faucet to rinse my hand, and I noticed that the blood had stopped running down my hand. Right before my eyes my freshly cut hand had closed up and healed! "What the hell just happened!?" I shouted. I shut the door and closed the blinds and sat with my back against the wall. I looked at my hand again for a few minutes; the shirt I was wearing was newly stained with my blood, but there were no remains of my wound. I opened my drawer and grabbed a clean shirt. I threw it on the bed and removed my clothes, I jumped into the shower and took a seat. The shower was my favorite place to be when I needed to think. I poured a glass of scotch and pondered back to the first day I had arrived. The low muttering that was barely recognizable to the human ear. The history book with the coincidence of one of the school's founders bearing the same name as father, the airport with only evening flights and blood banks and the black blur that was strong enough to knock me on my ass in passing. I took a huge gulp of Johnny Walker hoping that the alcohol would numb my brain so that I could block out my newly branded memories. Headmaster Phalanx's instant change in appearance is what was most disturbing to me. What was inside of her that came out? What was it about my blood that set her off so much that she demanded I leave at once? I poured another glass and thought, [laughing]; no way could it be. Was my theory so obnoxious that I could disregard it? Of course not, what was different about me that when injured I could rapidly heal?

During lunch, I sat in the corner and listened to my iPod. Florence and the Machine tuned the loud chatter in the room out. Karen Cartright walked into the cafeteria reading a novel. I think she was reading Ann Rice's "The Vampire Lestat." As she walked she read. I turned off my music and decided to meet her halfway. "You know you shouldn't read and walk; it isn't the safest thing to do with your temperament," I said jokingly. "Oh?" Karen replied. "Well yeah, what if you bump into someone as I did to you? You may go blowing up on people." I said. "You know Mr. Shrinewald; you make a valid point. I'll make a note of that for future reference." Karen said smiling. "So what's Lestat like?" I asked. "You know Ann Rice's novels?" Karen asked. "I know a few or so, and I'm a bit of a reader," I replied. "Very nice, what happened to your hand, did you bruise it or something?" Karen asked. "No, [laughing]; why would you ask that?" I replied. "Oh, nothing, it smells freshly healed. Your scent is stronger than normal." Karen said. "My scent is stronger than normal?" I asked. "Yes, everyone has a scent, and I happen to have an acute sense of smell, amongst other things," Karen replied. "Interesting, Karen I have a question for you," I said. "Fire away Mason." Said Karen. "What is this place?" I asked. "Mason, it's a school, [laughing] a costly one at that," Karen replied. "Seriously, I need for you to answer me, I'm starting to think I'm crazy. I feel like I'm having a horrible and long dream." I replied. "Mason, let you rest assured that this isn't make believe, and perhaps you need to get some rest, and lay off the scotch. It could be affecting your brain." Said Karen. Karen seemed to quickly dismiss my thoughts on this place, almost too fast. I knew there was something different about this school. The students who attend here were all well off, but strange. I don't know what it was about the other kids and me that granted us the opportunity to be here, but I intended to find out.

BEDTIME STORIES

At lunch, I grabbed my things and headed towards the door. I got an awkward feeling I was being watched. With the same pained look, Headmaster Phalanx stared at me from across the cafeteria with a look of suspicion drawn about her face. I turned back around and proceeded towards the door. I thought about the conversation that Karen and I had earlier that day. How did she know I had been drinking, and the incident concerning my hand? I needed a change of pace; it was Friday evening, so I booked a suite in the mountains about twenty miles south of campus. Cerival met me at Shriners Hall, he took my bag and placed it into the trunk. "Thank you, sir," I said. "Not a problem Master Shrinewald," Cerival replied. I looked back at the school campus as we made off towards our quarters for the weekend.

Cerival glanced at me through the rear-view mirror as I gazed out of my passenger window and contemplated. "You look troubled young sir. I presume you're still adjusting to the heavy workload?" Cerival asked. "Oh no, the workload is fine, there are other matters that trouble me at school," I replied. "Ah, I see, girl trouble! Well, I assure you young chap, your troubles have only begun in that department." [Laughs.] Cerival replied. "It's not that either Cerival, it's just, (I silenced myself for a moment to think about the right combination of words to come up with a question. I thought what the hell, Cerival may be of great use.) What do you know about this school, this place? Its entire aura is unusual." I asked. "This place, this school and its students who attend are special. You all are unlike any typical adolescent who walks this earth. Each of you is blessed with many gifts, but the downside is that they also bring about darkness. You youth have also inherited each of your clan's curses, by god some would deem them gifts." Cerival said. "What do you mean?" I asked. "Mason what I mean is that "Luce the School for the Gifted" is a supernatural school; a school where our kind discovers our gifts, learn to control and harness them. The misfortunate part of it is that some of us do not wish to use our gifts for the greater good.

Then there are those who can't accept what they are and

run from it." Said Cerival. "Is that what happened the other day at school on campus?" I asked. "Well, I'm uncertain but usually when the Troverters are around it isn't for anything pleasant." Said Cerival. "The Troverters?" I asked. "The Troverters are a sentinel being solely born with the innate ability to enforce laws of our kind. You can compare them to how the humans have police officers. The only difference is it would seem this breed of a supernatural being is solely born to enforce our laws, and to cause anguish for those who break them. The Phalanx Clan control the Troverters, so usually, anything that they handle was assigned to them by Headmaster Phalanx." Said Cerival. "Fleeing is against Luce's Code of Conduct, and it also risks the chance of exposing the rest of us. By a blood oath, the Phalanx Clan is sworn to protect our secrets, by any means necessary. However cruel and unusual their methods may seem, in a weird way we are indebted to them for protecting the secrets of past, present and future. Your father would feel differently regarding some of our unusual customs." Said Cerival. "What do you mean Cerival?" I asked. "Your father believes we can live amongst the humans coalesce. Nero never agreed or thought it a wise idea to hide. He believes in lingering souls." Said Cerival. "Nero doesn't feel like he died completely. He feels that if we died, then we wouldn't walk this earth anymore. Ha! Your father was a little different from the rest of us." Cerival responded. "So wait a minute, how is it that I live if my father is technically dead? Wouldn't that be physically impossible?" I asked. "Well technically yes, but there have been stories in the past of our kind mating with humans and the hybrid child possessing unique abilities. Most of our kind fears the unknown outcomes of these events so for over a century they've outlawed it. Your father has always been a respectable man in our world, so when he met your mother, he campaigned to have some of our laws amended." Said Cerival. "Nero was successful, and many vampires followed his actions. The only difference between them and him is he is a prime." Cerival said. "A prime?" I asked. "Primes are original breeds, born into vampirism, so he has never been human. They possess unique abilities like mind reading, compulsion, super senses, etc. Their bloodline isn't diluted by the human's bloodlines, instead, with each one born the bloodline lengthens, and they become more powerful. There is a period in our history where after the Human-Vampire act was signed genocide occurred, killing the majority of our kind. Those who remained were lucky or more powerful than the enemy. Devastated and feeling responsible Nero left and went into hiding. He hasn't been seen or heard from until he enrolled you here at Luce. Perhaps he feared others would crave revenge and attempt to end his life as well as his family's. Well, Mason, I'm done for now, I'll see you in the morning."

Cerival had given me an ear full, and the shock was too much to bear. The information he had given me put things into a more precise focus. My mind had been much too heavy even to attempt to fall asleep. Slowly taking in everything that Cerival had shared with me I picked up my phone and called father. It was a quarter to three in the morning; the first attempt went directly to voicemail. I hung up the phone; I picked up my phone again eager to know more about the secrets mother and father had kept from me all these years. I felt like now, more than ever, things in my life were becoming more evident. All the questions that briefly entered my mind now lingered, and I needed to know why they would try so hard to conceal these secrets from me. Other than being a bit freaked out about the possibilities of my unique abilities; I thought being half human and a half vampire could be pretty cool. Who knows maybe even use my gifts to my advantage; I wondered what gifts lie dormant inside me. Would I be able to use them to my advantage to get out of isolation for being late to class? Would I possess mind control and influence people to do whatever it was I wanted them to do? All these ideas made me smile in the way you did when the criminal committed a crime and got away scot-free. Was I thinking too far into it? Was that the kind of stuff that happened only in movies? My genetic makeup, perfect; symmetrically, physically, mentally and emotionally. I became more aware of my scent. Cerival mentioned how people would be lured in. He spoke of father's glory days when our kind still hunted. There was no longer a need to hunt humans anymore Cerival explained. There were enough blood banks in the world for our kind to survive and live a somewhat normal life. In layman's terms, I was the first known hybrid of our kind, and I liked it.

It was Monday again and the dead of September; I woke up, took a shower and continued with my morning routine. Lately, I felt sluggish, and I wanted to find a way to my boost my energy levels. I pulled open my MacBook and typed into the Google search engine, "ways to boost your energy levels." I waited a few seconds while the computer loaded. "Ah, here we are!" I shouted out rubbing my hands together. Web MD was the first option on the search engine. I clicked onto it; some ways that you can boost your energy levels are regularly exercising, proper nutrition, at least eight hours of sleep. All three I had regularly deprived myself of, well I had to change that. The moment I sat back in my chair, there was a knock on my door. "Who is it?" I yelled out. I opened the door after waiting a few moments for a reply. "An invitation?" I asked. It was an invitation plus one to a Black-Tie event this Saturday coming. I opened the invitation, and it read. "You are cordially invited to the 206th Annual Contrivers Ball." "Contrivers Ball, they have a group that dedicates themselves to lying?" I asked. "Talented misguiders, your and our kind like to call them, supposedly the Aura's cunning way of maintaining balance and keeping us on our toes," Karen said. "Karen, how did you," I asked being interrupted. "You still reek of scotch, so it's never difficult to find you." Karen interrupted. "Alright, a little strange," I said. "So it says here you have a plus one, sounds like an excuse to go shopping," Karen replied. "Oh, I don't know if we should be leaving the campus at this hour, besides I don't know if it's in my budget," I said. "Mason, your driver drives you around in a fancy car. Most first-year students can't afford or aren't allowed their own drivers until their third year; it ensures they don't drop out. Also considering that there is a building built in the memory of your father, I'd assume the Shrinewald Clan is doing alright." Karen replied. "Alright, but we can't be gone long, I have tons of work to do," I said. "Fair enough, I'll have you back in good time," Karen replied. We pulled up to the mall and parked her 2015 Lotus Elise and proceeded to walk towards the main entrance. "You know, for someone who's accusing me of being loaded you sure have a nice car." I pointed out. "Correction, my parents, are loaded, and I only benefit from it as long as I attend this school. Hell if I had it my way I'd live out of hotels and travel from state to state. As always my parents didn't think that was a sensible way for a Cartright to live. They seem always to find a way to sabotage my plans for my life." Says Karen. "I'm sorry to hear that; one of our parents was applying so much pressure, and the other never applying enough. Mother and father always allowed me to sort of linger within myself." I replied.

"Well let's change the subject off of parents; my parents depress me way too often. So, how did you come to receive an invitation to the Contrivers Ball?" Karen asked. "I don't know, it was taped to my door when I opened it, then a few seconds later you came," I replied. "Mason, the Contrivers is an organization of overly talented deceivers. They're extremely gifted at persuasion, and it's a big deal because they seldom invite people who aren't apart of their organization to their events. They've invited you for a reason, Mason." Karen said. "So what are you saying?" I asked. "They must want you to join their organization. It's been rumored for decades that your clan, the Shrinewalds, are born with their abilities but choose not to use them." Karen replied. "What do you mean?" I asked. "Haven't you heard your clan's history before?" Karen asked. "No…" I replied. "Mason, the Shrinewalds are one of the most feared clans in the world, but all they have brought in the past is good. The Contrivers must be inviting you to join to use you against the other prime clans. A Shrinewald as Contriver would change a myriad of events. They must think you're pretty badass huh?" Karen asked. "Do you think I should go?" I asked. "Sure, why not? Be careful;

these people have a way of toying with our emotions."
Said Karen. "Will you come with me?" I asked. "Didn't I
mention I have a gown I've been dying to break into?"
Karen replied. "So we're on?" I asked. "We're on baby!"
Karen yelled out.

During class, I daydreamed about what the Contrivers
would look and be like. They would probably be old
snobby men and women; people who only spoke about
themselves and money. "Pay attention Mason, and we
have a test on this material tomorrow." Regis interrupted. "Regis how could anyone listen to Mr. Ramble speak,
his mouth moves so fast, and he talks so low." I
asked. "You know Mason, you've got a point, but
somehow we all understand, and most of my notes are
dead on with what he's taught us in class." Said
Regis. "Man I'm just out of it today, and it's been a long
past couple of days. First, my family history was more
than I bargained for, then a knock at my door and there
was this black invitation in this unknown fancy writing."
I said. "Are you crazy!" Regis whispered loudly. "What's
the matter with you?" I asked. "Put that away before
someone sees you!" Regis said. "It's an envelope, Regis," I
replied. "Mason that isn't an invitation to a party, it's a
Contrivers invite!" "I'm aware of that," I replied. "Mason, Contrivers is a secret society of exclusively talented
and gifted people. Very powerful these people are and
very seldom do they recruit as well. Their supernatural

abilities far surpass the ordinary kind of any student attending here. They have highly concentrated abilities; they're filled with heirlooms that descend from primes! Are you getting the big picture?" Regis asked. "Are you saying they're like a supernatural cult?" I asked. "More or less yes, but far worse and way more dangerous; they act and lash out on others with no motive. They are strategically reckless, and their emotions are impulsive." Regis replied. "This ball I've been invited to, do you think it would be a good idea to go? What's the worse that could happen if I just went and looked around a bit and learned a little about them?" I asked. "Mason you have to be careful, this isn't just any school, there are a lot of unnatural beings around here. Indeed, you are a Shrinewald, but their advantage over you right now is experience. They'll all appear to be young and festive, but Contrivers always have hidden agendas. The only issue is finding what that hidden agenda is." Said Regis "I've already discovered one of my tricks, let's see what else transpires." I replied.

After class, I met Karen at Lunar Hall for lunch and to go over plans for the Contrivers Ball. Karen and I had somehow grown attached to one another; not an emotional way but in a way that best friends were. I enjoyed her company because it was like she could read my mind. Karen spoke my thoughts before I did; she was caring, spontaneous, intelligent and adventurous. Her curiosity level was relatively close to mines, but everything else about her mirrored me and I liked that I could be myself around her. "Do you like your eggs scrambled or over easy?" Karen asked. "Eww, I don't like eggs," I said. "Hmph, ok well what about oatmeal, I have tons of that?" Said Karen. "Not in the mood for oatmeal," I replied. "Ok, so what are you in the mood for picky one!?" Karen asked. "Don't look at me strangely, but I typically eat rare steaks, extremely rare or a half cooked chicken," I replied. "Eww, gross!!! That doesn't make you sick?" Karen asked. "No, it makes me feel nourished and energized." I said, "Well I'm not eating anymore, I've lost my appetite." Said Karen. "So let's get out of here, the day has just begun, classes have come to an end, and the big ball is tomorrow," I said.

The ball was tomorrow, and it seemed as if the day ran like molasses. People wandered around the campus having picnics, playing basketball and listening to music. Karen, Regis and I sat on my deck and sipped Heinekens and people watched. "You mentioned briefly to me the other day something about an Aura," I said. "Yeah, I did, what about it?" Karen responded. "Well you mentioned what it was but you never really elaborated on it," I said. "Alright; [laughs] see the Aura is what humans know as the atmosphere. The elements so to speak, except for the elements have a purpose." Said Karen. "What purpose might that be?" I asked. "As the sun exposes your kind and reveals what you truly are, so does the moon to my kind in which it exposes us to be well, um well let's just say they create an even playing field for all of us humans and supernatural alike." Said Karen. "Noted," I said. Karen had done well at summarizing what the aura was, but she had begun to pull back when she began talking about herself. I knew there were things about Karen that she has hesitated to tell me, but I'd just decided I'd wait her out. "Alright this is like my fifth beer and all the writing is in German. Who in America sells German beer written in German? Don't they know you Americans typically only speak one language?" [laughing.] Says, Regis. "I don't care about the bottle, and I'm only concerned with what's inside of the bottle," I replied. "Just a thought." Regis said, "Hey, and how do you even know it's German?" I asked. "Well for starters I lived in Brussels for five years and two I'm a voice." Said Regis. "A voice, alright I'm gonna need you to build on that Regis," I said. "A voice is a special breed of human beings who can read and speak any language. We also serve as vessels for apparitions who have passed on." Said Regis. "So wait, you're like an interpreter for humans and supernatural beings alike? I asked. "Precisely, occasionally an apparition gets comfortable and tries to occupy our bodies permanently, and when that happens, we have removals performed. Humans know them as exorcisms." Said Regis. "What do you do when that happens?" I asked. "I call on my clan to help remove the spirit. The deadly thing is that if the spirit occupies our body for a long period, my soul weakens and it then becomes their body forever." Says Regis. "That's nuts," I replied. "Yeah, in most clans vesselling is frowned upon but sometimes necessary although it is dangerous." Said Regis. "Vesselling, an interesting term," I noted. "Have you ever seen Ghost, with Patrick Swayze and Demi Moore?" "Of course I have seen that movie," I said. "Well, vesselling is like how Patrick Swayze and other ghosts could jump into other people's bodies." Said Regis. "So you're a voice, I'm half vampire half human, Karen why are you here?" I asked. "Excuse me? Because you invited me over, Mason." [shakes her head.] Karen answering the question sarcastically. "I'm sorry I didn't mean it like that, I meant why are you at this school. You haven't told us what makes you so special. What gifts do you have?" I asked. "I wouldn't call it a gift, more like a curse," Karen replied. "Ah, so that's why you bunk at Lunar Hall, like that was a surprise." Says Regis. "Don't worry, I won't say anything; I'll let you share when you're ready. Mother Knight has always told stories about how timely your kind is. No pun intended Karen." Says Regis. "What is it Karen? There's nothing to be ashamed of, tell me." I said. "That's easy for you to say, you're born with all the tools of seduction and weaponry. I'd just rather not talk about it right now ok? I haven't really accepted it all that much myself." Karen replied. "Alright, well whenever you're ready to share, let me know," I replied. "Alright." Said Karen.

What could be so wrong about Karen's clan and their abilities that she would hold it inside even if it killed her? Well, I couldn't afford to think too far into her logic; the Contrivers Ball was tomorrow, and I needed rest. "You two can hang around if you like but I'm gonna attempt to get some sleep," I replied. "Wouldn't want the bloody tricksters to catch you slipping now would we?" Regis shouted facetiously. "No, we won't have any of that stuff going on," I replied.

CONTRIVERS BALL

*T*he morning came sooner than later, and I felt an anxious sort of way. It was Saturday morning, and I decided to linger around my dorm. I mainly spent the day watching black and white films and cartoons. To the right of me, I was accompanied by my favorite drink Johnny Walker Blue. I sifted through my phone and logged onto Facebook and clicked on my events tab. I found the flyer for the Contrivers Ball. I didn't understand how it made sense to advertise an event that you could only attend through invitation. Perhaps it was their way of making their notions public so that they may seem harmless, and that notion in itself appeared blatantly intentional. My head suddenly felt light, and the sunlight bothered my eyes, I felt weak suddenly. I reverted to my newfound information that I

retained in the mountains and with Cerival as well as my
Web MD nutritional guide. I sprung up off of the couch
and walked to the fridge. I opened up a raw steak placed
it onto my plate and proceeded back toward my sofa and
cartoons. Minutes passed as my nausea faded away.
Perhaps the blood inside of the steak made me feel better.
I was still getting the hang of this newfound lifestyle my
parents had neglected to mention to me. Still curious
about my supernatural abilities I wondered when my
gifts would surface. The bathroom was one of my
favorite places to relax. The jazz, the hot water and the
humid atmosphere made for my kind of relaxing situation. The Contrivers Ball had finally arrived, and I felt
like I was on the edge of my seat being tormented by the
unknown suspense building up. My tuxedo had been dry
cleaned and firmly pressed, my shoes had been shined as
well, and I was ready to rock. I turned off the water from
the shower dried off and walked around my room. I
reached for the lotion first then I reached for my Chanel
cologne and sprayed a few sprays. I walked into my
bedroom and noticed that I had five missed calls. Two of
which were unknown, the other three were calls from
Karen. I picked up the phone to call Karen, and just then
the phone rang again, I picked up.

"Mason why aren't you dressed yet, the ball starts in
one hour, and it will probably take us roughly forty-five
minutes to get there." Says Karen. "I'll be ready, should I

call Cerival and have him get the car ready?" I asked. "No that won't be necessary, I'll drive you around this evening; we'll have fun, and it'll be a riot!" Karen replies. "Ha! I hope so; I'm a little weirded out by this evening, I feel like something's going to go wrong." I said. "Mason it'll be fine, you should be thrilled that you can put to rest all this suspense. I mean, just think, you are a potential candidate for the Contrivers. That's badass!" Karen yelled excited. "Karen you seem to be far more excited than I am," I replied. "Well Mason, I'm outside, and I have some scotch to loosen you up, let's go!" [honks horn.] Karen replied.

The evening bore a chill unlike any other I had felt before. Karen's Lotus seemed to set a trail of leaves that followed us through the night. The trees peered at us in passing; crows congregated and crowed cacophonous sounds. Tonight seemed obvious, it looked like the setting of the entire evening would be intentional. The atmosphere lay heavy with fog, and I could barely see the moon. "You haven't touched your drink," Karen said. "Oh, I'm sorry, I was just taking in the evening, tonight feels very day of the dead like," I responded. "Quite an imagi-nation you have there Mason, this isn't a horror flick. Drink and shut up, you're killing my buzz." Said Karen, as she shifted into third gear. [laughing.] "That was very direct." I replied. As much as Karen was sassy and direct; I liked it, in fact, it turned me on in a way, although I'd never allow her to know that for the benefit of her plea-sure. "Ha! We're here! This is the address correct? 1117 Linwood Lane?" Karen asked slowing down as she pulled up at the gate. "Correct Ms. Cartright, shall we proceed to the gate, or make a run for it now?" I replied. "I wouldn't miss this event for the world! I've heard boogie man stories about these Contrivers; besides wait until I tell my friends and family that I was a guest at the Great Contrivers Ball. They will glow with jealousy and envy." Said Karen. "So, is that the only reason you came with me to this event?" I asked probing for more reasons. "Mason, even when a girl tells all, she won't ever truly tell you all she's thinking. You may use that to your advan-tage, and that I cannot afford; at least not now." Karen replied grimly smiling. "Well put, perhaps I should pay more attention to your actions and less to your words," I said. "Maybe you should," Karen replied. When we pulled up to the gates, there was a painted mixture of black and purple. The colossal house sat on a hill with large panes that boasted the contents that resided inside. Two tall fully cloaked men stood at the gates; only their ruby lit eyes were visible. Already anxious I tried not to focus on their eyes. "May the recipient speak his full name so that we may know he is viable?" The cloaked man asked. "Mason Shrinewald" I replied. A sudden flicker in his ruby lit eyes and hesitation to speak alarmed me. "Is there an issue with the invitation?" I asked. "No issue, you may pass." Said the cloaked man. "That was a bit stranger than I'm accustomed to; this is like something you see in one of those Harry Potter Flicks!" Karen sarcastically said.

We got to a large circle where valets took Karen's car, and two more cloaked men stood like statues at the door as they opened them up simultaneously. Classical music echoed through the house blended with the loud chatter. A look of curiosity, excitement and seclusion stirred about Karen's face. I'm not sure how she knew how to respond to the environment. "Good evening Ms. Cartright, I do not know if I have ever had a member of the Cartright Clan attend one of our balls. I'm certain this evening will be memorable." Said the grim voice. "Good evening sir and you are?" Karen asked. "How rude of me, I must have misplaced my manners somewhere back there. I am Marius Griswald." Said Marius "Quite an event your organization has put together this evening." Said Karen. "Well, I'm glad that you are enjoying yourself. It was my turn to have the event at my home, so I was responsible for all the decorating and planning. So, Karen, tell me, where is your friend Mason Shrinewald?" Marius asked. "Mason Shrinewald, [Mason extends his hand to shake Marius's hand.] "Marius Griswald, nice to meet you," Marius said. "So, Mr. Griswald this is a fine establishment you have here; may I assume your clan owns this home?" I asked. "Yes, it is safe to assume that; it's been in my clan for quite some time now. Through the ages, each heir has added their own little touch to the house." Says Marius. "I see, quite the collection the Griswalds have of antique statues here," I replied. "Ha, they aren't antiques Mason, those are my family members petrified. So, I would ear to the side of caution of calling them relics." Marius responded. "I see, so what exactly is the purpose of this annual event Marius?" I asked. "Well it's complicated, but to sum it up every so often we run across exceptional talented individuals and uh; it would be foolish of us not to follow suit," Marius replied. "When you say follow suit," I asked being interrupted. "Mason, I mean we are a worldwide organization that focuses on improving our elite and making them that much rarer." Says Marius. "So you're a group who already has money, power, respect and grand accomplishments, who strives to take even more for one another?" I asked. "Precisely Mason," Marius replied. "Ha Ha Ha Ha" I laughed. "Do you find me amusing?" Marius asks annoyed. "Oh yes I do, and I also find it pretty disgusting that someone who has everything can relentlessly aspire to take all that they can with no remorse," Mason replies. "Well, Mason those who are equipped to adapt will do just that and those who can't will perish." Says Marius. "Oh, I get it, the survival of the fittest mentality. You should try your beliefs out on those who equal you, see how it works out." I taunted. "Say, that doesn't sound like a bad idea, even the snobbish fellows every so often needs a beating! I wouldn't mind a wrapping at my chamber door." Says Marius. "Well, be careful you never know who'll answer Marius," I replied. "Heed your own advice Mr. Shrinewald; now if you'll excuse me, I have a party to host." Marius races off furious. "I see Marius danced all over those buttons of yours, and I don't think I've ever seen you worked up. Except for the one time I sat on your lap. [Laughing], never mind that, let's go get a cocktail." Karen said.

Marius had struck nerves I never knew were there until just a moment ago; I didn't like it. Marius Griswald was a tall, slender fellow with a deep melanin skin tone. I believe his eyes were gray, he had perfect posture and stood 6'5, and he spoke with a deep resonance in his voice. Very forward his way of thinking seemed to be as if you ever had to guess about what he intended to do or say. Through our brief interaction through conversation, there was one thing I was sure of, I did not like him. "Perhaps you should try going with the grain for once Mr. Shrinewald, and you spend too much time going against it," Karen said. In my peripheral, I noticed that Marius and Lady Phalanx were conversing. "Lady Phalanx, it's a surprise seeing you here," I said. "Is it Mason, why would it be such a surprise that I would be in attendance at the Contriver's Ball?" Lady Phalanx asked. "I don't know I guess because I assumed it would be limited to those who were invited and members," I replied. "Oh, I see, well

Marius is an associate of mines, and the Phalanx clan have been partners for decades." Said Lady Phalanx "Partners, Partners in what?" I asked. "Let's say the Griswald Clan and Phalanx clan have a common goal and we are now closer to it than ever before in fulfilling that dream. You enjoy your night Mr. Shrinewald, Ms. Cartright." "Yes, Lady Phalanx," Karen replied. "Yes." Said Lady Phalanx. "Nice dress." Said Karen. "Thank you." Said Lady Phalanx. "She seemed more pleasant than usual, that was awkward." Says Karen. "Well let's get out of here, I'm sure we can find something a little more entertaining than dining with snobs," I said. "I agree, let's get out of here." Says Karen.

KILLER INSTINCT

$\mathcal{T}$he night was humid, and the street lamps were dimly lit. There was a fog that made the straight path opaque. It was quiet, silent to the point of where it was an apparent empty sound. "It's a lovely night, and we should go for a walk over the bridge," Karen says. "Well, Karen it just so happens that I am in a strolling mood, so I extend to you my arm, shall we?" I added. Karen and I walked, and we talked the evening away. She always set me at ease with her stimulating topics we discussed. She kept me guessing about just how interesting she was. Karen asked me a question about my decision in joining the Contrivers. I evaded the question and grabbed her hand as I commented how big and beautiful the moon was.

"Ouch!" Karen yelled. "What's the matter, did something bite you?" I asked. "No," she snatched her hand away. "Mason, what kind of ring is that?" Karen asked. "It's a sterling silver family ring given to me by my father," I said. "I think I'm allergic to that metal, and my skin is on fire," Karen said. "Look at that moon it's so bright, I didn't know tonight was a full moon with all those clouds out earlier," I said. "A f-full moon?" Karen asked. "Beautiful isn't it? Yeah look at it, it's full as ever, is there a problem Karen?" I asked. "Mason we have to go, we have to go now!" Karen yelled. "But we just got here what" [interrupted] "Oh no, you're not going anywhere." Said the masked man. Three masked men stood around us, my heart sped up, and my hands began to shake. It was obvious they meant us harm. "What do you want from us?" Karen muttered. "Well, for starters your money, then your life. You privileged beings think you can waltz into our town, go where ever and take whatever you like? Don't you think they'll be consequences for your kind? You practically have the world handed to you! Tonight you will only embrace one last thing from our hand, and that will be DEATH!" Said the masked man. "AAAAAHHHHHHHHHHH! It hurts, it hurts so bad!" Karen yelled, folded up and began to scream in agony. "Mason go!" Karen yelled. "I won't leave you, Karen," I yelled. "Well there sweetie you don't look too good, looks like someone done beat us to the sweets!" Said the masked man. Karen was in excruciating pain, her eyes tightly shut, right hand on her right side of her stomach while her left hand clenched the ground. Her body began to swell quickly, Karen drenched in sweat and her body temperature permeating off of her physique. "Mason make it stop; please make it stop, please make it stop! Karen cried. "Karen what can I do, what's happening to you?" I asked. One of the strange men grabbed Mason by his neck and dragged him back to the other men. "Now where were we young man, let's see, ah yes that's right I was in the middle of taking your life!" The masked man said. "Ahhhh! I can't fight it anymore, Mason run, I don't want you to see me like this.

I c-can't fight it anymore, oooooooowwwwwl!" Karen said. Karen curled up into a ball and one by one her limbs began breaking and dislocating. Her dress ripped as she grew in size. Karen's white hair color had now covered her entire body as fur; her face slowly disfigured as she grew a snout. Two sets of oversized teeth protruded from her mouth. Her jade eyes once dim now grew bright; Karen was a white wolf. Karen leaned back and sprung forward toward one of the strange man's minions. "AH-HHHH! Help me, Help me! Don't let it take me pplease!"

The minion screamed. The masked man stood his ground petrified, uncertain of whether to move or be still. "Get back! I have your friend. I'll tear his throat out if you move an inch, I'm not bluffing, I'll do it!" The masked man screamed. "Ah, but of course you will. Do it,

I have no use for a Shrinewald, for he would surely end my life the first opportunity he gets. Indeed he's gorgeous none the less, but the true killer elite of us all is MASON SHRINEWALD!!! KILL HIM NOW!" Karen yelled. A baffled look upon his face, unclear of what just happened, the strange man began looking at Karen and then looking back at me. My teeth porcelain white now razor sharp sneered at the strange man, and his eyes grew black as night. I had surprised our false aggressor, who now became the victim.

"NOOOOOO!!!!!" screamed the masked man. The masked man's screams had echoed through the air. In the midst of conversation, Lady Phalanx paused. "The cobblestone straight away, send Troverters, now!!!!" Lady Phalanx yelled. My instincts had taken over; that weekend in the mountains Cerival had told me that when an enemy posed an immediate threat that my killer instinct would take over and protect me. It would be like I was a different person, and perhaps this is why I had been so guarded my entire life. For years my mother and father did extra to keep me out of harm's way. Having Cerival to come to my aide whenever I called, but this time Cerival was nowhere to be found. I grabbed the man's hand and broke away from his hand. All in one movement I sprung up and drove my hand through his chest. When I retracted my hand, I held the man's heart. "The human anatomy, a heart... still beating, I didn't know you had one." I said smiling sadistically. "Now you my kind sir, whatever shall I decide to do with you?" "Please no, please don't hurt me! I was only following orders, please!" Said the third minion. "Orders? Orders from whom?" I asked. "I'm only an initiate, please don't kill me!" The third Minion replied. "Now, now, calm yourself, all I want to know is who would feel it fit to send someone to attack my friend and me," I asked holding the minion's face. "I can't say anything, or he'll kill me!" Said the Minion. "SSSSHHHH, then there's no reason for you to carry on!" I replied by breaking his neck. "Mother was right about you Shrinewalds; you're quite the killers." Said Karen. "Karen, Karen, Karen, for someone unstable and as violent as you are, you're one to point fingers." [Coming back to his normal state] "Three men just tried to kill us or me, and I-I don't know how it happened I just reacted. This is crazy, Cerival told me that when I was in danger, I'd respond a specific way, but he never mentioned acute killer instincts!" I cried. "Haven't you wondered why you react to things so naturally? Is there any doubt in your mind as to why you can adjust to almost any situation? You have gifts Mason, one of which is extremely rare for our supernatural kind, adaptability. Most of us are created to dwell in certain environments, you on the other hand… What's that noise?!" Karen replied. The calamity augmented as time flew by, between me trying to figure out what was coming and Karen's prattling I distanced myself. "Do you hear that Mason, they're coming for us; turn off your defensive mechanism so that they may never know who we are, we don't have much time to decide. I can sense your skepticism; and if I were here to hurt you, I would have already tried to kill you. Mason, we have to run!" Karen said. In the blink of an eye, Mason and Karen were gone.

[On the phone] "Yes sir I know I-, yes sir I know. I don't have an excuse as to why I didn't catch the perpetrators. Of course sir I know, I apologize this isn't my normal performance. Yes, master, I'll make sure I get down to the bottom of this Master." Said the Troverter.

EVEN IF IT KILLS ME

$\mathcal{N}$ ext week in school the days progressed slowly; classes seemed to be twice as long, and I seemed to feel twice as tired. I needed to hunt; my newfound blood thirst gave me issues. I had no self-control over my thirst, anything red only teased me. The myriad of scents in a room reminded me of 30 varieties of a boundless supply of heroin. The cravings came at the same time daily. For several weeks I isolated myself; the incident that happened the night of the Contrivers Ball couldn't happen again. I was a natural-born killer, and it scared me. I stared outside my dorm window and watched the leaves blow in unison. Flashbacks haunted me; could I be traumatized by my instincts that lay dormant?

[Bzzzz.] The doorbell rang, but I tried to ignore it.

[Bzzzzzzz] Whoever it was, was persistent and knew I was home, so I walked over to the door and answered it. "Haven't seen you in a while." Said Karen. "Uhh, I've been uhh…" I replied. "Busy?" Karen interrupted. "MMMmmm… not quite. I've been trying to fight this newfound bloodlust. Each time I gather a scent of a human my senses go wild." I replied. "Mason, don't fight what you are, learn how to moderate your cravings and control it. The longer you put off accepting what you are, the longer it will take you to come to grips with it." Said Karen. "What are your plans for the evening Mason?" Karen asked. "As far as I know I don't have any plans, why do you ask?" I asked. "I have an idea…" Karen said. "Yeah, well what is it?" I asked. "Well it's a full moon tonight, and I figured we could kill a few birds with one stone," Karen replied. "Ok?" I replied. "The Cartright Clan has been having issues with hunting parties at night vandalizing and ruining our crops. If my facts are correct, there should be dozens there tonight. We can go hunt; the objective for me is to send a message to the party that I do not welcome them on our land, and your objective is control. Mason it will only take a pint of blood to keep your health up. Restraint isn't easy, but it can only be conquered through practice. Most of your kind only get bad reps through blood lusters. I will help you practice control even if it kills me." Said Karen.

"Even if it kills me." the last words Karen spoke

between her and me yesterday evening. Why would she feel so strongly about my success as a killer? Had Karen caught feelings for me? Perhaps she feels responsible for me since she knows of the abilities of my kind? Was our bloodlust that detrimental to the human population? I decided tonight while we hunted I'd come right out and ask her. Karen pulled up in front of my dorm at approximately 11 pm. Her eyes glimmered with hints of silver and blue in the irises but mainly jade. Perhaps it was the black she wore that augmented the allure of her eyes. "You look stunning," I said. "I'm dressed casual Mason," Karen replied laughing. "All the same stunning, is the drive there long?" I asked as I got into the car. "Not really, but we will only drive half way and then travel the rest on foot," Karen replied. "On foot, are you serious?" I asked. "Can't have anyone seeing my vehicle, and remember we're traveling onto my Clans land, so we have to tread lightly." Said Karen. "Fair enough, so even if it kills you, what was that all about?" I asked. "Long story Mason," Karen replied. "Well seeing that half of our journey will be on foot; we've got the time," I said. "I knew someone before you of your kind. You remind me of him immensely, and the only difference is he became a blood luster. He found out the hard way what he was. Nile was abandoned by his clan, and he had no one. Back in my earlier days I was so caught up in denial with what I was that I abandoned him just as his clan did. The

Troverters captured and killed Nile. Nile begged for my help, and I refused. I feel responsible for his death. After that day I made a promise that if a friend needed me, I would be there until the end. Even if it kills me, you see Mason; you're kind is a very dangerous species, however; if guided you can be a useful force of nature. We're here; stay behind me and do as I do." Karen said. [Whispering] "Karen what if I can't control myself?" I asked. "Mason you have to try at least, don't focus on the negatives. I need you to focus Mason; when I turn, you'll be on your own for a bit. It's important that you remain focused Mason. This is an exercise of willpower but it is also real, this isn't tactics class. You won't have time to think about every move. Trust your instincts Mason, but be cognoscente of your natural bloodlust. You will be powerful beyond measure if you can master constraint of your natural bloodlust. Now when I say go, I will head for the woods and remain there until I change." Said Karen. "All right, I'll take the high ground and formulate a plan," I said. "Fair enough Mason, be careful," Karen said.

My hunter instincts were taking over once again. Only this time I was more aware of my surroundings; each scent in the open field I could identify. The night seemed brighter; like night vision. My eyes felt as if they were a flashlight turned on and beaming into my eyes into the night. I could hear anxious pulses as if there was a beating drum right beside my ear.   I tried to tune it out, but the night seemed filled with calamity. [Is Victor sure that this is the Cartright Clan's land?] Thoughts from the thief. I looked around to see who was addressing me, but no one was there.   What in the hell was happening? [Oh my God it's freezing out here, this is the last time I'll take another job from Victor; he's always so secretive, and he constantly has us in a heap of weird-ness.] Thoughts from the thief.   I focused my eyes on one man whose facial expressions matched the words I kept hearing.   Could it be I possessed mind-reading abilities? [Sounds like something is lurking in the trees, this Twilighty crazy shit! Mental note to self; never answer Victor's phone calls again. Hell; I should just delete his number and change mines although his gigs pay so well. I know I need the money.] Thought the thief. Two trees stood further than the rest of them. I braced myself to prepare to jump onto the next branch... [There's some-thing in those trees; are those black eyes?! What in the hell is that!?] Thought the thief. Just as I jumped the thief peers up at the trees with his night vision scope.   Damn, I've been made- "I have movement in the tree men; I'm southbound in the Cartright Clans land; come quickly I am not certain what level of threat this creative, maybe!" Says the thief. Just as the thief turned on his infrared beam to aim at me; I lunged back and sprung two trees forward. BBBBBBBBBBBBLLLLLLLAAAAATTTTT, BLAT,

BLAT! Several rounds had been fired; I leapt forward again only to have more shots dispersed. "He's heading east! Cut him off by the left river bank." Said the thief. I had jumped down from the tree and jolted toward the barn; by the time I had got there, I noticed that several men were cutting off every way toward the woods. I stood petrified for a moment trying to surmise my next strategy so that my next move would not be a fatal one for them. SHICK! SHICK! Assault rifles cocked, and red beams are pointed directly at my forehead and chest. "I presume you are the latest addition to the late great legendary Shrinewald Clan eh? Ha, Ha, Ha, you don't have to answer that; I've heard horror stories about your Clan. However, none of the Shrinewald Clan members appears threatening. Boys, we all know looks can be deceiving." "You all should leave before it's too late!" I warned. "Ha Ha Ha Ha Ha; do you think you're in any position to make any demands? You're captured at gunpoint, and alone! There have been rumors that the Phalanx Clan have taken extreme measures to procure the perfect primes blood; could you be the missing link?!

  Hey fellas, take a peek at Sara's new shiny toy!" That would explain the blood banks around the city offering various incentives for donations. "Mason, it is Mason, right? Ha, I'm going to kill you, but it will be a pristine death; we haven't come here for you. I have a job, and I cannot allow you to interfere with my business affairs. I am certain a Shrinewald; such a prestigious Clan understand the value of being a man of your word?" Asked the thief. "Who are you?" I asked. "Mr. Shrinewald; right now who I am is not important. Light the torches!" The thief yelled, "Don't do that, I'm warning you the consequences will be severe!" I warned. "Ha, right." The thief laughed. HOOOOWWWWL! [Karen howling.] "Right on time, what kind of party would this be if we didn't have a member from the lovely Cartright Clan? Switch to your silver magazines! Mason, I'm enjoying our little chat, I really am, but I've a job to do." The thief said. SMOCK!!!! The thief strikes me to the ground and launches the first torch toward the barn. The thief then proceeds to throw the other torches toward the barn to burn up the Cartright Clan's land. One of the henchmen cocks the rifle and demands that I get up. "Get up Shrinewald," Says one of the thieves. "What do you want from me?" I asked. "What does everyone want from you? I WANT YOUR BLOOD!!! It has been rumored that your bloodline is the key to supreme superiority over the elites. I want to dominate over the PRIMES! Imagine, no more dummy missions, no more chastising and no longer will the feeling of inferiority linger!" Said the thief. "Are you insane?! How are you even certain that I am the answer to the questions you so long awaited for?!" I asked. The henchmen seemed apprehensive and uncertain of whether he should engage to retrieve my blood or flee the scene.

I could hear his pulse dancing inside of his chest; I listened to his sweat trickle down his skin like the sound of a rockslide. I rendered his blood circulating throughout each and every vein in his body, this man was blatantly afraid. I reflected back to what Karen had said, restraint is essential; my hands began to shake, my mouth began to salivate. I could feel my eyes glaze over into a blush red. My teeth protruded past my upper lip. I reached out to clinch the predator now a victim. My teeth penetrated his skin with ease and once again; a new line of bloodlust flirted with me. The taste of my victim's blood taunted me to end him, but constant reminders of me not wanting to be a monster sent my feed into an abrupt seizure. As blood ran down my lip, I could feel my strength increasing, my weakness fading away from me. "STEP AWAY!!!" BLAT, BLAT, BLAT! Silver bullets from a semi-automatic rifle had breached my right forearm, but my clench remained strong. Un-affected but irritated by the thief's futile assault, I crushed his partner's larynx and ran towards him. I could hear his thoughts of fear sprinting through my head, and then suddenly there was a white flash. FWOOM!!! Karen had fully transformed and stood over the gunmen as she opened her mouth to rip out his throat.

"I'm surprised you saved so many for me Mason." Said

Karen. "I thought, we were practicing restraint? Mason
replied. "Well Mason we are but who gets anything right
the first time around?" Karen replied. "My sentiments
exactly Ms. Cartright," Says Lady Phalanx. "Lady
Phalanx! What are you doing?" Asked Karen being interrupted. "I staged this entire operation; I am the reason
why they are here, why you are here! Do you think
trained professionals would waste so much time
attempting to kill two of the world's most deadly supernatural creatures?" Asked Lady Phalanx. "Why are you
doing this?" Karen asked. "Ms. Cartright in every world
there is a requirement for order, the Phalanx Clan is that
order. Ha. Without us, many causes and reasons to go on
would perish." Said Lady Phalanx "Let me guess, and it's
your solemn duty to uphold and enforce what it is our
clan can and cannot do?" I asked. "Like it or not Mason,
there are people all throughout society that play the "bad
guy" every day so that you can enjoy the luxuries of
having your freedom. Who do you think protects your
precious clans and covenants? Ah, I see your wheels spinning Mason; right about now you're probably wondering
what is being noble truly worth? Who really notices the
deeds of the noble? Only time will expose the answers
to these questions." Lady Phalanx answered. "Lady
Phalanx; this kid can't be trusted we must exterminate
him now!" Said the henchmen. "NO ONE IS TO
TOUCH MASON; but Ms. Cartright, do what you will

with her." Lady Phalanx replied. "Mark me when I say this, and mark me clearly; the first to lay hands on Karen will face a slow, assured death by my hand." I threatened. "Why protect your natural enemy? Centuries ago the Cartrights and the Shrinewalds commonly fought one another. To loathe her is a part of your DNA." Said Lady Phalanx. "Not anymore it isn't," I replied. "There are too many of us to fight all of us, Mason." The Henchmen cried. "All the same sir; my abilities to bring death seem to come quite reflexively. I suggest you not take your chances and find out what tonight will bring you…" I replied. I looked at Karen as she stared back at me; my emotions had expressed themselves tonight. "Mason this is foolish stop this at once, your destiny has been written clearly in stone. Which way you decide to go is solely up to you, you pose an immediate threat to the humans as well as all the supernatural breeds as each day grows wild. Eventually, you will have to choose; you don't see the full picture yet." Said Lady Phalanx. "There will come a time when you will come to me in dire need. The Phalanx Clan are the ones that keep everyone's secrets. We're done here; let's go, gentlemen, drill over." Said Lady Phalanx.

Tonight I composed myself, tonight I didn't drift off into the deep end. Karen had left me alone long enough for me to repeatedly give into my bloodlust temptation.

There were many questions inside of my head that frustrated me; I needed to know the answers. There was only a hand full of people who could address these questions. I picked up my phone to summon Cerival, the night was long, and I needed rest; but I also needed to see father. "Cervial, ready the car, yes, yes I'm alright. No, I don't need a ride now Cerival. I need to speak with father. Yes Cerival, right, I'll see you soon. Oh and Cerival, bring two blood bags for me to consume." [I hang up the phone.] When Karen and I returned to campus Cerival had already been there waiting for me, he waited in the car while I showered and changed my clothes. With each day my senses amplified themselves somehow; my cravings augmented as well. I picked up the phone to decide whether I should inform my parents that I would be coming home for the weekend. I placed my phone back into my inside pocket, grabbed my weekend bag and left out my dormitory door.

Cerival met me at the car door to open it and shut it after I had entered. "Thank you, sir," I said. "You're welcome young sir. Is there anything else I can provide to make your ride more comfortable?" Cerival asked. "Yes please, blood and scotch on the rocks," I replied. "Coming right up, Master Shrinewald," Cerival replied. I leaned back into my chair, put a Santogold cd into the player and placed on my Ray Bans. "I'm such a lady, I'm such a lady," song ran through my head as I contemplated about my decision to protect Karen at any costs. I began to wonder about if I needed her would she do the same for me. The answer I came up with was yes. I recollected back to when she told me that she would try her best to help me get control of my bloodlust. "Even if it kills me", the most caring words she had spoke to me. I began to wonder about how she felt about me. Would it be too much to come right out and ask her how she felt about me? Would that be awkward? Would it change our relationship with each other as friends? Did I really care to find out? I sent her text asking, "are you good?" Karen replied, "Yeah I'm good." I responded "good, I'll see you soon." "Not soon enough" Karen replied with a smiley face. "Goodnight," I replied back. I didn't want to make it blatantly obvious that I cared about her immensely; although it probably wasn't hard to tell. I had made up my mind that she and I had each other. The car slowed down as Cervial got off at exit 53. "Even if it kills me." The phrase made me smile.

WHAT AM I?

We arrived nine minutes before midnight and pulled into the driveway. Cerival opened my door, and I walked up the driveway and proceeded towards the front door. The house was warm and cinnamon scented aromatherapy candles lit up the foyer. I could hear music coming from father's office blended with the swift pecking of father's laptop. I approached his door and stood there for roughly five minutes. Hesitant to disturb him. "I'm sure you didn't come all the way from school to stand outside my office door unannounced; you may come in son." Said Nero "Hello father, I didn't want to disturb you." I said. "Mason you may speak what it is on your mind; speak swiftly though, I have to prepare my proposal for tomorrow evening." Said Nero "Father, what am I?" I asked "Mason, you're a young man who needs to sort his life out; time isn't on our side. Be sure of yourself and move swiftly." Nero replied "Is time not on our side father? Father, what am I and why are we so different?" I asked "Well higher income brackets hardly would qualify us as" "FATHER! Why do I crave blood? Why can I heal within seconds of being injured? Why do I have trouble sleeping at night? Why is it so simple for me to kill people, yes KILL! Yes, I have killed men. These things are beyond normal, so father, please answer me when I ask you, WHAT AM I?!" I yelled.

"Nero I heard screaming from down the hall, and it sounded like Mason's, Mason what are you doing home from school? Is everything alright?" Mona asked. "Mother, father, were you two ever going to tell me? For the past few months, I have been struggling to maintain my composure, fighting my lust for blood, dangling by a very thin thread on whether not to drain people of blood. It all makes sense to me now, why you two never age, why you won't eat any of the food you cook, why you two sent me to this school; and for what, to find myself? Why couldn't you tell me?" I asked, "Mason, we were going to tell you." Mona replied. "When, when I decided to go on an uncontrollable blood lusting rampage? I am hanging on by a very thin thread! I need some answers; I need you two to help me through this. I am uncertain on how much more I can take." I replied "I know what you're going through, and I know that we haven't been honest with you Mason; understand that any reasons were to protect the Clan. In my earlier years of this life, I was naïve in believing I could sway all our kind to view the world as I did. Many people suffered for my actions; many still do." Nero replied.

"Father, what happened that was so awful that you hid me from myself? Did you think it would be that simple to cover your tracks? You've always been a prominent individual; you cast a large shadow father. All the time while at school I often hear and read about the things you've done for our school. The opportunities you've created for our kind. After all of that why go into hiding?" I said. "We left Baton Rouge before you were born because I feared our kind would come after you for revenge. For centuries it was forbidden for our kind to procreate with the humans. When I met your mother, she was human; for years we kept our love a secret to keep us both safe. The Human Vampire Act had not yet been passed; the vampire laws forbade our kind and humans from procreating because they feared that it would not only dilute the pure breeds, but it would also enhance it in ways that have never been seen before. I grew weary of your mother and I hiding our love so I began to advocate and amend our laws so that vampires and humans could coexist and get married. My peers at first resisted but with each attempt, they grew tired and gave in. Many of our kind came to the surface and followed my decision to love a human being. Unlike me some were incapable of defending themselves against the vampires who still believed that humans served only one purpose; to be our food. Many of our kind grew angry and went on a rampage. The "Nocturnal Cleansing" of our kind they called it. Not long after your mother became pregnant with you; I left my seat as a council leader and professor at Luce, and we left town. After you were born, I turned your mother into a vampire to ensure her safety. It was not a simple decision to come back to Baton Rouge and enroll you in the school, but I knew the school could help you. I knew that things would be different once we returned. My greatest accomplishments were now my greatest failures. I planned it over and over in my head to sit you down and explain everything, but I could never bring myself to it. Mason I've failed you and I'm sorry for that son." Said Nero.

"Mason please know that our decision wasn't an easy one. We did what we deemed necessary to keep you as safe as possible. I knew that one day this predicament would arrive, however; I fear our issues are only beginning." Said Mona. "Mother what do you mean our issues are just beginning? What you two did was for the well being of our Clan." I replied. "Mason we changed how it was to live in secret amongst humans as a vampire. The old way of life for our kind is now finished; vampires don't do well with change." Said, Mona. "So what about all the things the movies say about us? Like how we can't survive in sunlight?" I asked, "That's a myth son; we appear a little different in the sunlight, but I am quite fond of sunlight." Nero replied "Crosses, stakes, silver all of that jazz." I said. "Crosses don't do anything, stakes are a load of crock, however, some of us have allergic reactions to silver and white gold." Nero replied, "Ah, I see." I said.

"So son, what other questions do you have for us?" Nero asked "How do you control your lust for blood? All I think about is blood when I'm around humans." I said. "It takes practice and discipline, the human part of you will initially conflict with your cravings and what you've known your entire life. Your vampire traits lay dormant until your initial interaction with blood. It is similar to a switch that is difficult to turn off. Vampirism is a curse, but we can find beauty in even the most wretched things in life. I will teach you how to control your thirst, harness your gifts and refocus your emotions which will now become amplified since you've had your first taste of human blood. I will also show you the appropriate measures to take to ensure you get the proper amount of rest. Mason, it is true that we are oddities of nature; but humans and vampires can coexist. It's been my belief since before you were born and that belief remains. Tonight we will hunt; I will show you alternatives to surviving as a vampire." Said Nero. I knew tonight would be awkward; but if I had a chance of being some-what normal in the world, I'd have to learn to control my bloodlust. Tonight would be the night that father would teach me how to hunt.

THE THIRST

*T*he night was unexpressed; I could hear and see everything. My breaths got heavy for a moment, and I began to panic. Suddenly every sound cluttered my ears and made it difficult to concentrate. "Focus Mason; although difficult this is a necessary skill for a successful killer. The longer you dwell in a tempting uncontrolled state, the more likely it is that you will lose control and give in to the bloodlust. This is when our kind makes mistakes." Said Nero "Got it, ah there's one, he smells delicious should I go after him?" I asked "Mason, quickly you want to hunt but not recklessly and foolishly. Observe your environment; be sure of the risk factors in the surroundings of your prey. Believe it or not, there are still people out there who wish to end us Mason; so be careful.

"Your mother tells me you're a gifted thought reader. Do you see her there?" Nero asked. "Yes, yes I see her, but she doesn't smell appealing, which means she'll probably taste awful." I said. "Lesson #2, remember, we feed to survive, and eating is not to entertain or to be appealing. If it is a practical, safe and low-risk meal, engage." Nero said. The girl was intoxicated and aimlessly walking down back streets in downtown Baton Rouge. We followed her down a dark alley where she had reached into her purse to grab her flask. I strolled above her on the rooftop reading her thoughts. Girl's thoughts: [I always pick the wrong guys, I hate that about me. He said he loved me; maybe I'm not pretty enough. I'm going to hurry home so that I can use that blade I just bought on myself. It hurts but any pain would be less painful than how I feel right now. I want this pain to go away.] The girl said. She apparently doesn't think highly of herself and has self-esteem issues. I felt bad, but the time was right, I had to strike. I thought if I talked to her, that I'd feel better about killing her. I jumped down off of the roof in front of her. She stopped to gather herself and instead backed onto a dark brown brick wall and slouched down to the ground while crying frantically. I stopped to observe her for a moment longer when father said. "Mason what are you waiting for, ATTACK!" Nero yelled, "You're a good person, don't let him get you down; you'll be fine." I came closer to comfort her; she took two steps back and gasped for air to prepare to scream. My hand now wrapped around her neck to silence her and pull her close and sunk my teeth into her neck. I could hear father speaking inside my head [Mason, you've had enough, you can stop now...] I didn't want to stop. I kept feeding; [Mason stop...] as bad as she reeked of alcohol, her blood was borderline addicting, and I could not stop. Her heart began to slow down. Her panting decreased minute by minute, and her pulse began to fade. All in one stroke father was now by my side, but it was too late. Her heart had stopped, she was gone. "Mason, does a human have a conversation with their steak before they consume it? Never have compassion for your prey, it makes you weak!" Nero said angrily "I'm sorry father, she was so depressed and inebriated, I didn't know what to do or say." I said.

Her name was Amy Laurington, she was 19 and from Baton Rouge, as I was. I took her school I.D. and stared at her face well into the next day. Study hall was long and drawn out. I wondered if Amy had any friends; of course, she did, what kind of young girl didn't have any friends? Did Amy have a family, perhaps they had become worried and gone looking for her? I was a killer with a conscience; would I feel this guilty after every victim I fed on? Father had made valid points back in the alley last night. He made valid points about hunting and feeding being a necessity, but I hated that I took the life of such a young girl to preserve my own. I decided that I would seek out other alternatives to ensure my survival. "Who's the dame?" Regis asked as he sat down beside me. "Just some girl I met once." I replied, "It's kind of strange to be carrying around her school I.D. don't ya think?" Said Regis. "No, she doesn't need it anymore," I replied nonchalantly "Ha, right she's probably looking for it right now." Said Regis "No, she doesn't need it anymore because I killed her last night." I replied "Mason, you say that like it, like it was easy. What, you're some sort of serial killer now!?" Regis replied. "Regis, leave it alone because you don't know the facts," I said. "No, I don't know the facts, but I know you've been rather aloof lately. Why haven't you been around, I thought we were friends Mason?!" Regis replied "Regis I'll explain things in time; right now all I can say is that I've been in a difficult bind and I'm working at controlling my urges. This vampire lifestyle hasn't been easy for me. Ever since I've tasted blood, nothing has been the same. Food has no taste, hell I can't even keep food down unless it's raw red meat or chicken. My senses are all in a frenzy. This is a lot for me, not to mention it's new to me." I said. "Don't lose yourself Mason; I've seen how you vampires get once you've become addicted to the taste of blood. You become untamable and vile. I would hate to see my dear friend become some sort of blood fiend." Said Regis. "My father has been helping me come to grips with what I am.

I feel like a killer with a conscience [laughs]. I mean look at me, what kind of killer walks around with evidence of his victims on him?" I said shaking my head.

"Mason there are some parts of you that obviously sustain your humanity. The part of you that reminds you that you have a conscience and the girl you killed had a life. That girl somewhere has a mother, a father perhaps even some siblings. Grandfather Knight used to tell me many stories of the self-control your clan had; I'm sorry has. You'll get there, and I'm sure at some point your father had the same issues you have." Said Regis. Unlike me, father was born a vampire, and it would be difficult to see him not having control of his situations. "Control yourself, take only what you need," the phrase that consistently ran through my head each time I hunted. I decided to take what father and Karen taught me and apply it tonight; only this time I decided to hunt alone.

THE DILEMMA

J wandered the streets alone; looking for a lingering lost soul who would slip up so that I could satisfy my thirst. I came to a gentlemen's club where outside there stood a doorman. His physique was one of a football player on steroids; he had violet eyes and spoke very little. "What's the cover?" I asked, "I.D. please." The doorman replied. I smiled a bright and sinister grin; I looked him in the eye and said: "You don't need to see I.D., in fact, today's admission for all is free. Understood?" I asked. "Understood," the doorman replied and opened the door. Mind control; a useful tool I had been informed of when father and I went hunting.

I figured the more people inside of the club; the easier it would be to select my next victim. The music blared, and there was a thick cloud of smoke in the air. My heightened senses made everything overwhelming. I noticed this one particular guy in the corner. He wasn't smiling, and he perused the crowd strategically. He kept his hands at waist level and bumped into several people. He was quick, but not that quick; he had pickpocketed each person that he had bumped into. Now he had begun walking toward me. I made my way to the bar and ordered scotch straight up. He watched me from roughly three feet away. I had found my victim for the night. I baited him to the men's room so that no one could see me. I ran the faucet water on hot until the mirror grew steamy. The man followed behind me and used the third urinal to the right of me. As he flushed, he walked toward the door, and I stepped in front of him. Just as he began to follow through with his pocket picking routine, I paused. "You know Nathan, it is Nathan correct? [Showing him his own I.D. card] By the way, what kind of criminal walks around with their I.D. on them anyway? You're good; ha ha ha, but not that good!" I said. I grabbed my new found victim by the throat and yoked him toward me. I fed on him until he was no more. Just as he dropped to the floor, the bathroom door sprung open. It was two teenagers who stood there in front of me. I sprung into hyper speed and fled the scene. Too frantic, I had forgotten to compel them to dismiss what they witnessed. A part of me was concerned, but the other half of me enjoyed the thought of someone knowing my secret. I imagined it would not be long before they spoke on what they saw. I also knew there would be consequences for reckless behavior. Perhaps I had come to grips with what I was too soon and it was too much. This time I felt justified in taking that man's life. He was a thief, and he didn't deserve to live. Someone who lived like that I'd kill again in a heartbeat; it was easy. Last night's encounter was a close one. If I was going to hunt, then I might want to consider being more cautious.

I returned to campus at roughly seven am. There was a man in a black hooded cloak standing by the door when I arrived. He bore a telegram with the Contriver's symbol imprinted on the seal. "Master Griswald would like your answer by the end of the week." Said the Guard. I took my jacket off and placed it in my closet. I removed my shoes and poured a drink as I opened the letter; it read:

Master Shrinewald,

It has been brought to my attention that you have new found challenges with accepting your nature. One of my guards has discovered that you are a genuine blood luster. As you know in our supernatural law my friend, this will not be tolerated in our world. There are two ways we may resolve this matter, join me and we can make your problems disappear. The other alternative is Lady Phalanx will assuredly address the issue in her own way. Mason, you make life much too difficult for your-self. You are royalty amongst your kind as well as other species. Should it be your issue that you are indeed unique amongst your kind, indeed not? Your parents even kept your identity from you, and for what? To ship you off to a school that will tame you? Master Shrinewald, I implore you to join me, and I will teach you how to harness your gifts. I will expect your answer by the end of the week, Mason. I am confident that you'll make the right decision.

Formally,

Marius Griswald

It was Wednesday evening, and I had until Sunday to devise a plan of what I would do about my predicament. I placed the telegram down onto my coffee table and took off my clothes and ran shower water. There was a trace of blood that lingered around my hands and lips. The hot water pressed against my face and the blood trickled down into the drain as the water diluted it. I grabbed the bar of Dove soap and lathered my entire body up. Just then I heard my phone vibrate on my bathroom sink. I drew back the shower curtain to see who it was that was calling me. The number looked familiar, but I couldn't think of whom exactly it was that had been calling me. After I rinsed off, then turned off the hot water, grabbed

my black towel and proceeded towards my bedroom.
There was a list of contacts above my desk, and the
number that appeared on my phone was the school's
phone number. I walked back to the bathroom to grab
my phone. There was a new voice message from the
school. I pressed play after entering my pin number and
began to listen. "Good morning Mr. Shrinewald, we've
missed your presence in class. You are to report to my
office so that we may discuss how you plan to amend this
issue as well as catch up on your work. Oh and Mr.
Shrinewald, your presence is required; this is not a
request. Good day to you." Said Lady Phalanx.

Headmaster Phalanx sounded adamant about this
meeting; I wondered if she had ulterior motives. Were
Marius's predictions coming true? I threw on some
clothes, grabbed my book bag and was out the door. I
walked across campus and saw Karen heading towards
her classroom building. I debated back and forth on
whether I should speak to her or not. I kept my distance
behind her for a moment. "Mason, I can still smell you a
mile away." Karen said, "Damn, you can always sense me,
how do you do that?" I asked "Mason, I'm a white wolf;
the crème de la crème. Just as you are distinct amongst
your kind; so are we. Some werewolves run ramped and
only turn on a full moon; then there are white wolves
that can change at will. The only difference is we are at
optimum strength when a full moon arrives. So how has

the hunt been treating you?" Karen asked. "It's been a little patchy; actually, I'm in a tight spot right now." I replied, "Umm what do you mean by that Mason?" Karen asked "Well, two kids caught me feeding the other night at the C-Bar and now I'm in a dilemma. Marius Griswald is pressuring me to join the Contrivers; he says if I join, he can make this problem go away. Head Master Phalanx wants to speak with me about the days of class I've been missing, but something tells me she has something else up her sleeve. I'm afraid that she's going to address the same predicament Marius has written to me about." I said, "Mason, be careful; I've known kids that have done similar things and were called in to meet with Lady Phalanx and have never been seen again." Karen replied. As soon as Karen said that I had a flashback of me witnessing the kids trying to flee from campus. The Troverters would be sure to show their faces soon.

I got to Mr Ramble's class about ten minutes late, I slowly cracked the door open and attempted to gently shut the door behind when the door made a loud noise. "ERRRRK!" "Mr. Shrinewald, so nice of you to join us, please sit down; I will speak to you later." Said Mr. Ramble "Yes sir." I replied. My life seemed to become more and more complicated by the minute. It was Friday, and I had two days remaining before I had to make a decision. My thirst had drawn me into this dilemma, and I had to do something about it. I pondered on speaking to father about the matter, but it was time I started taking more responsibility for my actions. Marius did make a valid point about me being able to contribute my gifts to the group. I felt constantly contained and tamed. Marius noted that he would show me how to harness my powers and to use them without causing mayhem. I needed another opinion on this matter, but I wanted it from a neutral source.

I decided to call Cerival up and ask to meet with him. I sat on the front steps of the Knox building and waited for him to arrive. I looked across the campus and wondered what the lives of the other students were like. They all seemed so carefree and unaffected by all the things that shouldn't matter. Perhaps their realities hadn't set in yet and time was still on their side. Time wasn't on mine in all the ways I needed time to be there for me. Time had taken two bottles of NOS and hyper-accelerated; if only time could slow down.

MASON'S MEETING

*M*oments later my car pulled up in front of the building. "Master Shrinewald, good day sir." Cerival Said "How are you Cerival? We must speak on a few things." I said, "Yes sir, what exactly do you require my opinion on?" Asked Cerival "Now before I speak on the matter I need to know that you'll be completely honest with me Cerival." I replied, "Of course Master Shrinewald, I'll try my best to help provide you with an answer." Said Cerival. "Alright, here goes nothing, I am stuck in between joining the Contrivers or possibly being eliminated by Head Master Lady Phalanx and her Troverters." I said, "Well why would you have two awful choices like that to make Mason?" Cerival asked. "I've attempted to hunt alone, and in the process of doing so, I've managed to make a terrible mess." I replied,

"Mason what have you done?" Cerival asked. "Two people discovered me in the middle of feeding on a victim. My bloodlust has gotten me into a jam. Sometimes I feel like I can't control it. It's like once I get a taste of blood inside my mouth, I can't stop myself. I become reckless and conspicuous, and I'm unaffected by my surroundings. Lately, it has gotten worse; I've missed class so that I'm not tempted to attack some of the humans. Their variety of scents touches my nose as I inhale the atmosphere and I'm turned on like a switch." I said.

"Surely there is something that you can do, other than the ill choices you have. You're new to this hunting business; perhaps we can go speak to Lady Phalanx and come up with a viable solution." Said Cerival "Something tells me that Headmaster Phalanx won't listen or speak to reason. Lady Phalanx has a history of solving our supernatural problems by eliminating them all together." I said. "This is true Mason, and perhaps time will expose more options that we may not see right away." Cerival replied, "Ha, there's that word that isn't quite my friend again, time." I said. Time wasn't on my side. Marius had been persistent in his attempts for me to join his cult of talented liars and long living humans. Why would he be so adamant that I join his society? Was a prime that necessary to change the tone in the supernatural world? I didn't know much about any other clan other than what father had told me. I knew Lady Phalanx was a vampire, and so was the Shrinewald Clan; but what was different about the two of us? I noticed that Sara Phalanx applied force to get things done, very rarely did her techniques entail finesse. "If the Contrivers are fighting this hard to get you to join, there must be a motive behind their efforts. They're highly intelligent and resourceful, they also usually don't engage in matters that won't benefit their cause." Said Cerival. "How can we find out what's up their sleeve?" I asked "I will speak to a few people I know who are closely linked with the Contrivers and I will learn what they know. Your parents should have also told you that bringing you back to Baton Rouge was a big deal in our world. Mona and Nero have always been bad with judgment calls, they've always downplayed every-thing." Said Cerival. "Yeah, I get the feeling they've been away for quite some time." I replied. "Mason, this could get ugly because there seems to be an underlying issue around here involving you. The scary part is that I don't think Lady Phalanx seeks to end you. You're much too important to the vampire species to get rid of you all together, and she knows that. Not to mention killing a prime is no simple task." Said Cerival. "Wait a minute, what do you mean killing a prime is no simple task?" I asked. "Well typically beheading and burning a vampire, werewolf, brares etc. is usually all it takes. When it comes to a prime it's a long drawn out process; and by the time you get to the next stage, they've more than likely regenerated. Once a prime regenerates you have to begin the exhausting process all over again." Said Cerival. "I see, what time is it?" I asked, "It's fifteen minutes to six." Cerival replied. "Oh damn, I have to meet with Lady Phalanx. I have to go, look we'll chat later about this. That's if you see me later!" I said.

My stomach began to twist into knots with each step I took towards the main building. If I believed in a god, this would be my moment of prayer. After all the things I've been through, I can't believe that this was the moment that made me feel on edge. The campus was barren and deserted; I figured at any moment a stray animal would come running or a tumbleweed would come blowing across the campus. "You look nervous Mason." Said Marius. "Ha, au contraire, never felt better Marius. What are you doing here? Wait let me guess; you've come to see whether or not I've decided on your attractive offer." I said. "Correct." Marius said moving closer to Mason. "Well the week hasn't ended yet, I still have time to decide Marius." I replied. "This is true; Mason we're not how people perceive us to be, I can assure you of that. Lady Phalanx won't make you the same offer." Said Marius. "Why do you even care so much about what choices I make?" I asked. "You see, one of the cool things about being a Contriver is your amplified perception of reality. Most don't believe in intangible things; however, we swear by the intangibles. They have assured things that remain consistent and will always be so." Marius replied, "And you seek to acquire me for what, your benefits?" I asked. "Oh, Mason you worry about too much about the minor details. The Phalanx Clan and even your Clan seek to tame you. I seek to unleash you, to refine you! For you have far too many gifts, too many to name. Mason one way or another you will be unleashed, it isn't in your nature to be controlled, to be tamed." Said Marius. "I have somewhere to be, as much as I'm enjoying our conversation, I have to go." I replied. "Mason! Remember this; there will come a time when the lines between what your kind call good and evil will become blurry. Then will you have your moment of truth, in your greatest time of need. You will feel alone, abandoned, not even your friends or family will be able to console you. I won't be there to say I told you so, but I will be there to teach you about yourself. Yes, it is true we are selfish talented humans. However, I am not a fool, so I offer my allegiance. You'll need it for what lies ahead, we all will." Said Marius. As much as I hated it, Marius had made valid points. He'd given me something to think about. What if Lady Phalanx and her Clan had planned to outlaw me or end me, what if there was some other insane reason on why she had been so insistent on me seeing her?

My vampire instincts were augmenting by the days;

my thirst was more controllable, I had even been resting regularly. Now the only obstacle that stood before me was my supernatural secret that now has gone public. I didn't know what to do about that, but it seemed Head-master Phalanx, and Marius did. I walked into her office and greeted her secretary. "Good evening; I'm Mason Shrinewald, I have an appointment to see Lady Phalanx." I said, "Of course, please take a seat and she'll be right with you." The Secretary replied, "Thank you." I replied.

THE OFFER

There was an awkward silence in the room; the secretary was apprehensive as she dialed the number on the phone. I could hear her pulse speed up, and as she answered the person on the other end of the phone, she looked up at me. Her perfume now blended with her sweat which freshly evaded her pores. Perhaps this woman was afraid of my capabilities. Perhaps she had somehow heard the short-lived fables of me being this reckless monster. With time on my hands, my mind wandered further and further away from reality. Then I looked back up at the piercing stare I could feel glaring through me. As I paused, it made perfect sense, the woman at the desk was afraid because she was human. Perhaps she thought I might lash out and have an episode inside of the building. Next, I heard a door open, and footsteps advance toward the waiting area.

"Mr. Shrinewald, are you ready?" Asked the personal assistant. "Yes mam, I am ready." I replied, "Lady Phalanx will see you now." The personal assistant replied, "Very well, let's do it." I replied. My clammy hands tugged my pockets as she walked me to the back. Why was I so nervous? "Mr. Shrinewald, so glad that you decided to come to speak with me; as you know, this is a delicate situation that we have on our hands. Luckily for the school, the Phalanx Clan is fully prepared and adept in dealing with delicate situations such as this." Said Lady Phalanx. "I'm sorry, I'm not quite certain I follow." I responded. "Mr. Shrinewald, there is no reason to play naïve. You and I are fully aware of what transpired off of this campus a week ago. Luce's law states that using your gifts in the midst of humans will not be tolerated." Said Lady Phalanx. "Well I assure you it was an honest mistake," I said. "Honest mistake? Mr. Shrinewald, are you aware of the damage your bloodthirst can cause? In our world mistakes are never minor; our actions distinguish the difference between life and death. Whether we contain ourselves for the benefits of others or blatantly rip apart humanity." Said Lady Phalanx "Yes ma'am, I understand." I replied "Do you, really? See, Mason I have an issue, a conflict so to speak. You see, normally in a situation like this, when someone has risked exposing us all, I'd call in the Troverters, and have that "situation" erased from our timeline. However, this situation is unique. Mason, you are unique, your potential is boundless. You're a prime, so you see; ending your breed is a tedious process, and we don't have time for that." Said Lady Phalanx. "So what exactly are you suggesting ma'am?" I asked "The truth is, I don't know what to do with you Mason; however, something must be done. To be blunt, you are a natural born killer with all the gifts that the ordinary breed would kill for. Do you recall the blood banks and the myriad of incentives for blood donating? Our clan has been looking for the missing key to the puzzle." Said Lady Phalanx. "What missing piece to the puzzle?" I asked. "Centuries ago, vampires were the dominant species on this earth. As time passed, so did nature. Vampires that once walked the earth as the sole supernatural species were now accompanied by werewolves, white wolves, brares, voices, etc. You see, nature had its course, and these different breeds have diluted our species. Mason you were conceived days before our laws were amended, and thanks to your father our world would never be the same again. For now, anyone following the amended laws would be killed. This is why one of the school's founding fathers Nero Shrinewald left; he left to ensure your safety and hoped that you could live an ordinary life. Mason, your father, is a prime, so he is difficult to end, but this wouldn't prove to be the case for any other clan. Many people died standing their ground for their beliefs which mirrored Nero's. Nero could take care of himself, but you were a baby, so he fled until you were grown. Mason, there are an endless amount of vampires looking for your father, the same people that would hurt you to get to him" Said Lady Phalanx "Woah wait a minute, didn't they understand the risks before making the choice they made? How is my father responsible for having his own beliefs on how our kind should live?" I replied, "Oh someone has to take the blame, and since he was the first to speak out, who better than your father?" Said Lady Phalanx. "Despite the load of crock, how convenient it is for you. I won't apologize for my actions or what I am. You crave power; I suppose the elements were just in making you basic. [Laughs] You claim to be this loyal gatekeeper, but I can smell a completely different agenda all over you. You stink, and you disgust me! You're no better than any of us, the only difference between you and me is that you are completely aware of what you're doing. You wish nothing but ill will. This meeting is over." [Laughs] "Ha, Mr. Shrinewald you have so much to learn about the world. I know more about you than you know about yourself. It was me who sent for you after patiently awaiting your Clan's return. I staged the student's escape on campus knowing you were nearby. Once he blew past you and knocked you on your ass, he cut your hand. I had the blood sample I needed, and I was correct; your blood is the missing key in our evolution. So Mason, this is my offer; you will not be killed, you will not be tortured, you will remain in attendance at Luce. Your punishment will endure as long as I need it to; you will be my personal blood bank. In a few weeks, there will be a Shaman arriving from Brazil and he will conduct the transfusion. Mason, you are right, I not only crave power for myself but for my entire clan. I seek to reproduce and convert my clan until the lot of us are more powerful than you primes. I will find a way to complete the blood transfusion process without diluting or losing any of the replicas features. You are a beautiful creature, and I will get what I want from you by any means necessary. Soon your genetic enigma will become mines; now you may go." Said Lady Phalanx. How crazy was she to think that I would allow her to steal my DNA? One of her was too much to bear, I couldn't imagine seeing a grand clan of her.

I vacated the building and headed towards my dorm. I pulled out my phone to check to see if I had any missed calls; I had 6 missed calls from Karen. Karen was concerned about Regis because she hadn't seen him in days. I barely even noticed due to my current predicament; I dialed her number. "Hey Karen, slow down I can barely understand you. You found a note where? Where are you now, alright, I'm on my way." I said hanging up the phone. I had never heard Karen so distraught, so the matter must have been serious. I unlocked my door and jumped into the shower; afterwards I put on my black hoodie with my black denims. We were practically going to be hunting, so as I learned in my tactics class I should dress comfortably and appropriately.

MASON'S FIRST TRIAL

*K*aren arrived outside of Shriners Hall and sent me a text saying she was outside. Karen was still worried but had finally calmed down from being frantic when she discovered the note. I opened the letter and began to read it, it said:

Hello,

As you have discovered your poly lingual friend has been abducted. There is only one thing we require of you to see him again. Bring us the young prime vampire they call Mason Shrinewald; there is a bounty on his head, and we would like to collect. Oh, and we've left you some goodies to make things interesting along the way. You'll find the first clue to finding Mr. Knight on Clive Mountain. Happy hunting!

The Other Party

"Clive Mountain, Clive Mountain, why does that place sound familiar?" I said. "That place sounds familiar because it is the place where untamed and uncivilized of all our kind resides. It is a condemned place that we shouldn't go to unprepared. It's far too dangerous. Although these beings are untamable and uncivilized, they have had years of practice on victims to harness their supernatural abilities." Karen said. "Well, how do we get prepared for something like this?" I asked "Mason you're a prime, and that helps, but we need someone who can show you how to use all of those gifts you have. It's been rumored that the elements gave humans special abilities so they may serve as teachers and mentors to the primes. The Contrivers and Primes once worked together in keeping our supernatural world safe." Karen said. "What happened, why don't they speak to one another anymore?" I asked. "I don't know, but there has to be someone we can ask," Karen replied.

It was all beginning to make sense; Marius Griswald knew this was coming. Marius knew that the Phalanx Clan intended to exterminate the other breeds. This is why he was so hung up on me joining; to bring things back to balance. As much as I didn't want to admit it, Marius was right, and at this very moment, I needed him. Marius could show me how to unlock my gifts so that we could overcome the Phalanx Clan and see Regis again. Regis's well being now lays in my hands, and I couldn't afford to let him down. Regis is a friend, and friends don't let other friends die. Karen and I headed toward Marius's house, the road was dark, and the sky was brightly lit with a full moon; on the radio played "Big Jet Plane" by Angus and Julia Stone. "I like this song." Said, Karen, while turning the radio up louder. I drank my scotch blended and disguised in an all natural Nantucket Nectars cranberry juice. The blend was perfect, just enough to calm my nerves. I noticed a tall, muscular sentinel like being standing directly in the center of the road. Its eyes reflected off of Karen's headlights and began to run toward the car. Karen came to an abrupt stop. "What the hell is that?" Karen asked. "Well I don't know what it is, but I assume that it wants to speak to us," I said. "I'm going to try and go around it," Karen replied. [Laughs] "And you think that'll work? I'm going to see what it wants." I said. "Mason, I DON'T THINK THAT'S A GOOD IDEA," Karen yelled. "Unless you have a better idea, we don't have many options, besides the clock is ticking, we need to find Regis!" I replied. "Be careful Mason, and even you can bleed," Karen said. I opened the car door and shut it behind me. "Wait here," I said to Karen. I took one more gulp of my Nantucket cocktail chucked it then walked cautiously toward the statuesque being. "Hello?" I said. No response, I could hear this thing breathing but still no movement or response. "You know, standing directly in the middle of the road...are you lost?" Are you lost, I could've asked a more intelligent question than that. "Are you the prime known as Mason Shrinewald?" The being asked. "Who wants to know, can I help you?" I replied "Target acquired"- SMOCK! Before I knew it, I was airborne from this beastly thing striking me with such a great force in the face. This demon-like being had horns like a Thoreau with red satin skin, its eyes were yellow, and it possessed oversized teeth and a black tongue. When it struck me, it felt as if it had struck me with a red-hot hammer. "MASON!!!" Karen screamed. "STAY THERE KAREN!!!!" I yelled. I slowly rose again; my head grew foggy, my eyes turned pitch black, my skin pale yellow as I lunged toward the creature. "So it's Mason you want or the other guy!" I said. SKRUP!!! My body felt like it was operating on autopilot. I grabbed the creature by its throat and squeezed. I stared it in the face as the light in its eyes dimmed. RAAA!!! The beast let out a high pitch scream as my hand attempted to wring life from its body. Arms now locked with the ugly beast, both of us struggled to overcome one another tumbling. Its blood now called out to me, and I could see its main artery pulsating through its neck. I must have broken its skin because there was blood on my hands and I could feel my eyes widen in a glaze with lust. Over-coming the red beast, I broke its arm and spun around to the back of it. Pulling its head to the right by grabbing its horn to expose the main artery; I felt my fangs lengthen as I sunk them into its neck. "AHHH!" The beast yelped out. Slowly the beast settled down as I sucked the life force out of it. The beast pulse decreased with each sip of blood that touched my tongue. The fight was over, the beast had given up, but I had continued to feed on it. I couldn't stop myself; my bloodlust was in total control. As I came to the last drop of its blood, the beast turned cold, and its skin grew black. PLOP! My grip released the beast's corpse, and it fell to the ground. I walked back towards the car. "Let's get out of here," I said wiping the beast's blood from my face.

"Don't get any of that creeps blood on my seats, Mason!" Said Karen, shifting into first gear as she pulled off. Within forty-five minutes we had arrived at Marius's house. Outside, as usual, there stood two armed men who stood still and quiet like statues. The guards opened the gates without any questions being asked as if they were expecting us. "In the night I hear them talk/the coldest story ever told/somewhere far along this road/ he lost his soul/ to a woman so heartless/" [Kanye West song plays on] "I enjoy listening to this song whenever lady trouble visits me. In my century of living Mason, Mr. West is one of my favorite painters of the truth. His gifts will always be his curse, like you and I. In the beginning my slowly aging physical makeup seemed to be a blessing, a gift; like the lot that you have but no! You and I, we are cursed to watch the ones we care about with all the power we possess suffer. We bare witness to their anguish daily, while we prevail and in essence appear to be unaffected by pain and draw closer to finding ourselves drifting closer to infinite solitude. Such a sad, sad song, Mason. Some are born to live and die, and some are born to suffer. We, you and I my friend are born to suffer. You've come here to ask me for my help in rescuing Master Knight correct? I hear you're an avid scotch drinker, would you care for a glass?" Marius asked. "How did you know?" I asked. "That you enjoy a good drink?" Marius asked. "About Regis," I replied. "Mason, haven't you noticed that the people around you seem to know more about you than you know about yourself? Doesn't that disturb you? You were bred intentionally to change lives, [laughs] as well as end them. Born on a full moon by the perfect breed, you are a Shrinewald. Their greatest possession, amongst so many people, so lethal and other clans are maliciously envious of your gifts, gifts they would kill for. Which brings me to my next topic; I hear there's a bounty on your head. You're going to come across some of the most gruesome monsters known to our kind, but the crazy part is your instincts will vanquish any monster's abilities. Sara Phalanx knows this, so she's spinning her wheels." Said Marius. "How do you know it's Phalanx, Marius?" I asked. "Mason, I am the seer in our world; it's my job to know, not to be favored amongst the many but to know these things. It is also common knowledge that the Phalanx clan has craved power for as long as I can remember. She longs for things to get back to the way it was before your father amended the laws before you were born." Said Marius

"How do you know all of this Marius?" I asked. "Well for starters my clan taught your clan how to use and harness their gifts. My father trained your father how to use his gifts. When Nero married your mother Mona, he turned her into a vampire. In the process of turning her and marrying a human, he had broken many laws, and this outraged the Phalanx Clan who once shared an alliance with the Contrivers; which meant that they could no longer control the outcome and the future of your race. Contrivers and Primes parted ways due to the tension between the various vampire clans. I've known about you since you were a child. My father has groomed me for this very moment, to train you. My father knew this day would come." Said Marius "I see." I said. "I noticed you came in with a few beauty marks huh. You must've run into your first trial." Said Marius "My first trial, wait did you send that beast to kill me? ARE YOU CRAZY?!" I said. "Relax Mason, it was necessary, I have to make sure you're ready for what lies ahead," Marius replied. "So this is a sick game for you?" I asked.

"No, no of course not, but on Clive Mountain, you will be faced with many feats; so I need to make sure you are prepared. That is why you came here right?" Asked Marius "Yes it is." I replied. "Very well, I can help you unlock parts of you that you've never seen; but you must remember with all my talents, I am still only human. I won't be of much help beyond showing you how to use the gifts you already have." Said Marius, "Alright, well what do I have to do to be ready?" I asked. "Yes about that, you went through my centaur like it was easy; he was one of my best guys. I also noticed you enjoy the company of a woman. Just so I know that won't be an issue, I've surmised a second test, a trial if you will. Meet me at Merriam's Brothel in one hour; someone as sugges- tive as you are to women should still be fully alert and aware." Said Marius "I'll be there." I replied.

THE TRIAL OF TEMPTATION

*K*aren and I left Marius approximately forty-five minutes after he went ahead. We gave ourselves fifteen minutes for anything that may happen between us leaving and arriving there. "Is this the place?" Asked Karen "141 Eastwick Boulevard?" I asked. "Yep, Merriam's Brothel, are you sure you wanna go in there?" Karen asked, "Karen I don't have much of a choice if we're going to see Regis again." Mason replied. "I'm certain there's another way for us to go get Regis. I'm not sure if we should be trusting Marius; he is a Contriver." Said Karen "You heard what Marius said back there about Clive Mountain. If we're going to have any chance of being successful in getting Regis we have to do this. I'm only a first-year student, and you're a second-year student; there isn't a lot you, and I know yet." I said.

"Alright; well I'll wait out here and keep a lookout for anything out of place." Said, Karen, [Laughs] That's not why you don't want to go in, is it?" I asked. "Of course it is, well no it's not; I'm not gonna watch those filthy broads feel you up; it's disgusting!" Karen said. "Aww, if I knew any better I'd say you care about me!" I said reaching over to pinch her cheek, then pausing for a moment and kissed her lips. Karen closed her eyes and kissed my lips back as she exhaled slowly. "Woah, so that's what that's like." Karen said smiling and biting her lip. "Yeah, well I supposed I'll slide up in this building now." I said while walking away. "Yeah, well I suppose it would be a good idea." Karen replied.

I closed the car door behind me and walked into the building. "The Motto" by Drake I could hear playing behind the closed doors; I also could hear moans and screams. At the desk, there was a basket filled with what I would assume were the customers' black cards. "May I help you?" The lady at the desk asked. "He's with me." Said the Mistress. "Ohh Marius was correct, I really do like you. More importantly; I am dying to know how you taste." Said the Mistress. "I'm- [interrupting Mason.] "Mason Shrinewald, you may only refer to me as Mistress this evening, follow me." Said the Mistress "I guess that's alright with me, maybe Marius gave me the wrong address." I replied. "Did he give you 141 Eastwick Boulevard?" Asked the Mistress "Yes, that is the address he gave me." I said. "Welcome to Merriam's Brothel, by the way; I'm Mistress Merriam." Said the Mistress. KA JOMP! The door shut and suddenly I had a frog in my throat, candles lit a fire, and the lights dimmed. "Mr. Shrinewald, would you like a massage?" The Mistress asked. "I don't have time to waste ma'am,- [interrupting him] "Mistress." Said the Mistress, correcting him "Mistress." I replied. "Very direct, I like that, but for what I'm about to do I want to take my time and make sure I get every, last, drop!" Said the Mistress, with a grim smirk. She walked closer toward me and pushed me down to a seat. The mistress then began to lower herself toward the floor, and she had somehow doubled herself as if there was another standing directly behind her. A warm moist sensation had come over me; the room got hotter and hotter, my head began spinning. The music faded into the background to drown out the noises and all that resonated in my head were a phrase of lyrics "what of the dollar you murder for/ is that the one fighting for your soul/or your brother's the one that you're running from/ but if you got money/ then fuck it cause I want some/". Kanye West's "Clique" played in the background. The second apparition of her somehow disappeared then reappeared behind me. A provocative sound she made in my ear, speaking a language that sounded like Aramaic. How I had acquired that knowledge frightened me. "B'aD Mak!" Said the Mistress's apparition. "I'm sorry Mistress

I don't follow." I replied. The apparition began breathing down my neck, basking in my scent licentiously. "B'aD Mak! Mmm, B'aD Mak!" The apparition repeated.

"You can gather the fact that she is speaking in a lost language, Aramaic; but you can't interpret what she's saying?" Marius asked "Marius where'd you- [interrupted by Marius.] "I'll tell you why you cannot interpret what she is saying to you Mason; you are brightly distracted. These women, these parasites are in the business of blood lusting. Once the lust of blood entrances you, you can no longer reason or process things logically. The only thing you long for, the substance you will yearn, is blood. Lust is a blinding element, and it consumes your rationale. If you're going to be successful in retrieving your friend Regis, you will need full complete focus. Oh, and what she's reiterating in your ear, the very reason she's hovering over your neck is that "B'ad Mak, is Aramaic for blood." Said Marius. The Mistress's apparition grew fangs that drew four inches from her mouth and proceeded to grab me by my neck. "AHHH!" I yelped. The Mistress's apparition had slightly broken into my skin; two drops trickled down my neck onto her lips as she licked her lips and closed her eyes and paused as her face turned to stone. "MMM KHal Ya A!" Said the apparition, meaning sweet. Fully aware I quickly converted into defensive mode. "No, no I believe the term you're looking for is bittersweet, this will be your last taste of blood.

Now face the end of your parasitical life." I said. In one motion I drew in the Mistress's apparition, without putting up a fight the Mistress rose and appeased me. "Do you see the difference? Lust and temptation are two beasts you will struggle with constantly; indeed you are a prime Mason, but you are also still partially human. Being partially human makes you still vulnerable to these creatures in some ways, and they've had plenty of practice.

On Clive Hill, this is only a fragment of the feats that await you. You will stand before some of the most beautiful creatures in the form of humans with the most divine blood circulating through their veins. There will also be the most unstable creatures in all of Baton Rouge. Keep this lesson from this trial with you always. Two down, one more remains." Said Marius, We walked out of the brothel and met Karen at her car; I removed the handkerchief and wiped the blood off of my neck. "Looks like you had a good time." Karen said, "Ha, how could you tell?" I replied, "Well for starters, your fly is unzipped." Karen said, "Oh, well this isn't what it looks like." I said. "Oh yeah, well what is it?" Karen asked. "It's awkward, I mean the Mistress's apparition was trying to uh, but it never happened I mean uh, I didn't let her. Ha, are you guys hot or is it just me?" I asked, "It's just you Mason, [laughing shaking her head] what a trial you had to endure." Karen replied "What a way you have with women Mason, and it's refreshing to know that you are flawed in some departments. I was beginning to think you were perfect." Says Marius. "Coming from a gifted liar, I'll take that as a compliment. Well, we should get going." I said.

THE FINAL TRIAL

he wind blew in my face as we drove toward Clive Mountain and made me ponder about what my last trial would consist of. I couldn't handle all the empty spaces in our conversation. I quickly thought of something to discuss. "So what's the plan?" I asked "Well once we get close enough we'll travel the rest of the way on foot. I have Regis's scent so we can track him through the mountains." Said Karen "Cool that should be simple enough." I replied. BLOOM! "What in the hell was that?" I asked "Sounded like one of my tires; damn it, DAMN IT! We'll have to foot it from here." Said, Karen. "Well, the good news is that we're only two miles away from the entrance of the Mountain." Marius replied, "That's great, and the bad news?" "Them!" Marius pointed. "Them? Them who?" Karen asked.

It was foggy tonight, but I hear at least five hunters up ahead approaching, and they were heavily armed, I could tell because they reeked of gunpowder. FEWMP! FEWMP! FEWMP! Several stakes darted past me. FEWMP! FEWMP! FEWMP! Catching the last one and sending it back with reprise SWOOP! Arghh! The last stake I launched back pierced the furthest hunter's heart as he dropped instantly. "JACOB! You bastard you; YOU KILLED MY BROTHER! " The other hunter screamed. Already five in front of him, he ran towards me as I grabbed his wrist clutching the gun in his hand and with one squeeze broke his wrist. AHHHH! The hunter's gun fell to the ground. Overwhelmed with pain, I had taken the fight out of him. I glanced over to see how Karen was doing, and she had already transformed into the radiant white wolf I had seen on the bridge that night. ZZZT! AARP! Another hunter had used some sort of electric pistol to paralyze Karen temporarily. "Hey! Wolf beater!" I yelled. "Oh, you must be the one we came for." Said the hunter with a grin trailing about his face "Perhaps I am, and they sent out only five guys to apprehend me? Oh well, five minus two, not enough." I replied arrogantly. "You're an arrogant little fella aren't ya?" Said the hunter. ZZZAT! The hunter attempted to paralyze me as he did Karen. I paused for a moment and continued to encroach upon my prey. "Ouch! [Pauses] tisk, tisk that wasn't nice; what is that mouth drenching smell…it's rather close. I never knew they made hunters so sweet." I said. Pulling out his pistol the hunter fires his entire clip into me. BLAM, BLAM, BLAM, BLAM, BLAM, click, click, click. Pulling out a stake to drive through my chest. SEMP! "Mmm, close…but my heart is a little more to the left. You know, to be a hunter you're unprepared and uneducated in the department. Let me guess, hunter intern?" [Laughing] I said sarcastically. "P, P, Please don't kill me, please. I'll leave; you'll get no more trouble out of me please!" Cried the hunter. "Come on, ssshhh; you're pathetic, die with some dignity, on your feet!" I said, pulling his neck to the side to expose his main artery. "P-Please, God no, please!" Cried the hunter. "Ah, god can't hear you, and now no longer can anyone else." I replied sinking my teeth into the hunter and draining him dry. "Now that was pleasant." I said, "Two men left!" Said Marius. Of the two hunters, one began walking slowly towards me attempting to sneak up on me. "NOPE, only one!" I said, using my fingertips and razor-sharp talon-like nails, I dismembered the hunter's head from his body while holding it as he walked over to the last hunter. "You there, I have a special job for you." I said, "W, what do you want me to do?!" The hunter asked in a terrified tone. "Give this message to your dreadful Lady Phalanx. Tell her that her time will come soon and gracefully, tell her that I won't end her quickly. It will be delayed, NOW BEAT IT!" I yelled.

The hunter carried the head as he ran off into the darkness. "They'll be sure to send more, and we should make our way toward the mountain." Said Marius "You're right, Karen are you alright." I asked. "I'm fine, and we should get going we've wasted enough time with that unexpected party." Said, Karen. The three of us gathered what little belongings we had in Karen's car and veered right off the road with the intention of traveling unnoticed. The leaves were cherry red as if they had been infected with some blood disease. The trees were pitch-black with a minor tinge of purple. As we made our way through the woods the trees grew thorns; eyes from the top of the trees glimmered down at us. A cacophony of groans and snarls echoed through the woods. How could such untamable and uncivilized creatures detest us when they lived on Clive Mountain?   It was clear that we were not welcomed. "Karen it might be a good idea for you to turn back into a wolf now, you'll be better protected that way." Said Marius "Alright, [transforming back into her white wolf form.] So Marius, how did you become a Contriver? I mean, you know so much about the supernatural species, but you don't speak about your society much. Tell us something about you all that we don't know." Said, Karen. "Well for starters, I was born into this society 100 years ago to date. I am fascinated by all of the exotic perilous creatures that either fancy themselves god-like or damn themselves because of how they were born. Like the both of you, I didn't choose this life; it was decided for me that I would be in this society from the womb. My father and mother in olden times were influential members of our community. Copernus Griswald was a professor at Luce School of the Gifted; father taught the elements. See back then Vampires and White Werewolves were more common, before the Cleansing. They had to learn what elements exposed what each species was, what was dangerous to the human race and what weakened you all. Father was the best professor in the southern region when it came to the elements. Despite our slow aging and long living you' think we'd be wiser, but father was still flawed. Father had a strong affection for Head Master Sara Phalanx, of course, this was long before she became Head Master." "WHAT?!" Karen and I said in unison "Yes, she was one of his first students. Sara Phalanx wasn't always a vile vampire, she was one of the first generations of vampires deprived of their prime abilities. Prime vampires have special powers apart from the normal vampires, and primes possess the abilities to read minds, influence peoples decision also known as compulsion. Prime vampires could practically rise over almost any threat, and more. Most of their survival instincts are as effortless as the act of us humans breathing. You see Mason, this is why Sara won't kill you; she envies you, hell she needs you. She wishes to steal your gifts and believes that the way of doing so is by stealing your blood and harvesting it. She's been on a rampage for decades looking for your rare breed so that she can have a Shaman perform a transfusion; she believes it will work." Said Marius. "Has this theory ever been tested, I mean what if it doesn't work?" I asked. "Then let's hope you apply your trials and schooling accordingly. Indeed you are extremely powerful, but Sara has experience on her side. The Phalanx clan are professional and very deadly killers. They're hunting for blood, literally." Said Marius "I see, and what about your mother, did she find out about your father and Sara?" Asked Karen. "Well, as a matter of fact she did; [laughing] Lexia Griswald was the one who passed the Human-Vampire Act." Said Marius "A woman's scorn?" Karen asked "I guess you could say that; father and Sara along with many others feared the blending of the species. They were afraid of the unknown outcome; they were afraid the council would not be able to control new breeds. Contrivers help sustain balance in the supernatural world between the breeds. We are the most intelligent so we can deceive and manipulate, make things tricky for the supernatural breeds. That was the way the elements made it an even playing field. So with all of the laws being amended, control would now be difficult to maintain. Ah, anyway enough storytelling; we should be keeping full attention ahead." Said Marius. How strange it was that the only reason I was allowed to be born was that Marius Griswald's mother, Lexia Griswald amended Vampire Laws out of spite? I presume payback is a sweet kick in the ass for the recipient.

NEBULOUS OPAQUE

[Mason!] Voice calling out. "What?" Looking around, I stood in front of our trio and I could hear a voice call out to me. "Hey did you two just hear someone call my name?" I asked. "Not us, you feeling alright?" Karen asked. "I'm fine, I know I'm not going crazy, someone called out to me." I said. [Mason!] Repeated the voice. "See again! I heard it as clear as the two of you standing here beside me now!" I said. "Pull yourself together, and keep your voice down, you'll draw attention to us!" Said Karen [Mason turn left! I can help you!] Said the voice. Pausing, looking around to see if I could sift through the creatures in the night searching for the voice of reason. "Wait a minute Mason, perhaps what you are hearing is shrouders' thoughts. He or she is allowing you and only you to hear them. This way not only will they remain concealed visually but audio-wise as well, pretty impressive." Said Marius.

"Very good Contriver, very good, you've seen my kind before?" Asked the shrouder from the trees. "I have, why have you come here, who sent you?" Asked Marius "I am a friend of Cerival Primus; I am Nebulous Opaque I am repaying a debt to him by helping you. I've heard horror stories about Clive Hill; but after seeing the new horrors of vampire hybrids capabilities, I believe there is a chance of finding your friend on the mountain." Said Nebulous "Ah, so you needed to see proof to know if my friend would be worth saving?" I asked. Rushing over to Nebulous, I lunged toward him as Nebulous vanished into thin air. "Where in the hell did he go!?" I ranted. Up in the tree barely noticeable, this beings skin is liquorice black, with cinnamon eyes; he walked upright and had an arm that connected to his lower back that acted as a tail. "Be still Shrinewald, I am here to help you; make no mistake about that, but Clive Mountain is a vile place. One of three suicidal places our kind rarely travels to. I watched the hunters back their attempt to apprehend you and that won't be the last time they'll try to end you. Sure you're a prime, but is your friend worth your life? I can get you all to the top of the mountain shrouded and unnoticed, but you'll be alone after that. The bounty hunting has already begun. The Phalanx Clan won't rest until they have delivered you to Lady Phalanx. The feat won't be an easy one."

Said Nebulous "Yeah, I keep hearing that." I said, glancing over to Marius "How can we be certain that we can trust you?" Karen asked "I gave Cerival my word that I would return the favor. Cerival has saved my skin more times than I care to remember. Shrouders keep their word; I don't particularly agree with the Human-Vampire Act because of the enigmas that come with it, however, if Cerival needs me to help you I will. Besides, the only person that has a real shot at surviving on foot is you, Mason." Said Nebulous "He's right; we have a slim chance of making it on foot, but not without at least Karen or myself getting hurt or killed." Said Marius. "Knowing that you still set out on this wild trek? What if it's you who orchestrated this entire thing?" Karen said "I assure you that none of this is my doing, I did business with Sara Phalanx by force. I never liked her and most certainly never trusted her. My father and she are partially part of the reason why things are the way they are now. I seek to mend that reality, I want to bring things back to somewhat of a normal state." Said Marius "Why wait so long, why now, why me?" I asked. "Why, because you are potentially the only prime who stood a chance against Sara Phalanx and her small army. Being a Shrinewald, I also knew if you were anything remotely close to what your father is, that you wouldn't stray from our focus. Your clan is extremely strong-willed and loyal. The primes I've run into over the years were rash, irrational, power and blood lusters; they were incapable of being like you Mason. As much as Sara Phalanx hates you, she cannot kill you because she needs your blood to attain the gifts, and you to create the empire she desires. Mason, it could only be you; I've waited a century for this moment, so why would I wait so long only to sabotage it?" Asked Marius. "Well put, point taken." I replied "OWWWWWL!" [sniff, sniff] "There's another wolf out there folks, look alive." Said Karen. "Karen you handle the wolf and we'll- [Nebulous interrupting Mason.] "NO! That's exactly what they would hope for, and we cannot separate, we must stay together." Said Nebulous. "He's right Mason if we're going to grab Regis we need to stick together." Said Marius. "Hold on to one another; I'm going to shroud us to the mountaintop. At no point of the shrouding should you let go of one another. If you do, you will be brought back down here." Said Nebulous. BRAAAMMMP!

Without any delay, a colossal gust of wind and a dark cloud surrounded us and took us straight up to the mountain top. The cloud was cold and moist, if there had ever been a being that had walked through a cloud, this was it. At the top of the mountain, a gate of about twenty feet towered over us. In the distance, there were huts in the form of pyramids. It only rained in scattered areas; a trail of fire ran beside the small river banks. Two moons illuminated the night, they overlapped one another; one was pitch-black, and the other was dimly lit. "Well, this is where my journey ends, and when yours begins. When you make it through, I'll be here to shroud you back. Be safe; oh and I've heard stories of a hybrid living on this mountain; extremely vile, a red wolf hybrid. There haven't been any sightings of her in decades. Be safe." Said Nebulous.

CLIVE MOUNTAIN

*W*ithin an instant, Nebulous had vanished and once again we were a trio in the dreary atmosphere left lingering in the night. I approached the gate and attempted to open without force, but it was no use. Transforming into the treacherous hybrid I was, I pried the gate open as if it were a sardine can. My vampire strength at times frightened me. I began to understand why it took Karen so long to come to grips with what she was. Most days I was ashamed of what I had discovered about myself since attending Luce; but the vampire side, the killer inside of me, embraced it with open arms.

"This way." Said Karen. Marius and I followed behind Karen, and her acute senses made it difficult for anything to pass by unnoticed. My admiration for Karen had grown since the beginning of the school year. Although Regis was her friend as well as mines, this wasn't her fight. Karen never left me alone to this supernatural life. The ground beneath us began to shake; silhouettes in the shadows paced back and forth, but they didn't approach. "Why would they stare at us but not attack; this was the moment that they had waited for why not attack?" I asked. "Because they are under my command Mason Shrinewald." Said the voice. "Who's there? You again?" I asked. "Those questions are not important, and you only need concern yourself with if you'll leave in one piece." The voice replied.

"I think it's an apparition Mason, and it's beginning to make sense why Regis was taken." Said Marius. "The human you have with you is far too intelligent for his and your good. Perhaps, you should rid yourself of him. Enlightened humans are far too dangerous to live such long, informed lives." The apparition said. "Mason I think this apparition is going to use Regis's body to walk the earth again! We have to make haste before it's too late before your friend Regis is gone!" Said Marius. "Well, what do you suggest we do?" I asked "The fire, the fire, I'm trying to remember what fire symbolized. Two moons, one dead and one new; think Marius think!" Rambled Marius. Marius brainstormed on a way we could distract the apparition while taking on his beasts.

His guess would be much better than mines. "To see the face, you must quicken the pace. Blood blends with the trail of a blaze of the creator's face. He comes and goes; evades the place and add blood to the trails to create the face. A voice must vessel a soul in relation of the one who creates the place/douse the flames in trails of blood to bring about the face, and in rare times a prime will walk about this place. This is the blood that will recreate a Banshee's face." Marius was reciting the memory of an olden Grimoire. "Of course, Sara Phalanx needed you up here for two reasons; to revive and transplant. To transplant an ancient prime's apparition, who jumps from voice to voice and also to steal your blood. Not only would your blood douse these flames but these lines would draw the samples she needs to duplicate your blood if the transfusion doesn't work." Marius said, "That's a cute riddle, so uh what do we do?" I asked. "Regis has to be in one of these huts; it seems far too simple to go in and retrieve him. There has to be some catch; the apparition can't harm you in his present form. Phalanx needs you alive so she can't harm you either." Said Marius. "Well, couldn't I just sniff him out and lead us right to him?" Karen asked, "Well the only problem with that is what if his scent is spread all throughout the land; it could lead us into a trap unless you could detect those as well." I said. "Very good, now you're thinking." Said Marius. "What was that!?" Karen asked, "What was what, what did you see Karen?" I asked "I don't know, but it looked like the silhouette of a guard coming out of the hut back there. He carried a weapon that looked like a blade in the shape of a downward facing crescent moon on a staff." Said Karen. "Does that ring any bells Marius?" I asked. "Sounds like some tomb guard weapon. What on earth could be guarded here on the mountain?" Marius asked. "I just saw him again! I can't believe you guys didn't see that." Said Karen.

"Keep calm Karen; well we're not going to find out much standing here with our thumbs up our asses, I'm going to check it out." I replied, "Mason, wait, we need a plan!" Said Marius. "One thing I've learned today is some things we can't plan. The best qualities I have are my instincts, so this time we do it my way." I said. I transformed into my altered beast defensive mode and lunged forward; the first booby trap was two stake fire. SHOON, SHOON! Swiftly advancing towards the first hut; I go to open the door. "INTRUDER! Attention to all guards Mason Shrinewald is dangerous, and please approach with," SWAT! "With extreme caution, you were going to say, I'm sure of it!" I said. "MASON SHRINEWALD! STAND DOWN." I was surrounded by what appeared to be a dozen guards; all were armed and deadly. I gazed around and paused with a grin. "MASON SHRINEWALD, STAND DOWN! YOU ARE OUTNUMBERED; THERE IS NO VICTORY FOR YOU

HERE!" Said the guard. "Marius we have to help him! He's extremely outnumbered!" Said Karen. "Outnumbered? I don't know, [laughs] I'd say we are evenly matched!" I said as I pulled my first victim towards me and bit his throat out as the cipher of guards swarmed me. "Karen this might be a good time for us to go get Regis. It seems they've only provided enough guards to accommodate Mason. He'll serve as a good decoy, he can handle himself." Said Marius. "So what's the plan, there at least a dozen huts on this mountain and Regis could be in any one of them," Karen replied. "I'd say it would cut down our time since you're familiar with Regis's scent even though it's been planted everywhere," Marius said. "I should've tried this earlier, and I should be able to detect any booby traps they have planted in this place as well; stay behind me." Said Karen. Karen and Marius now began to sift through the mountain in search of Regis. Successfully avoiding traps until they reached the back of the mountain, Karen had miscalculated her last step and pressed on a stone firmly planted in the ground. "Oh my." Said Karen. "Oh my? Oh my doesn't sound good, what just happened?" Marius asked. "I think I just sprung a trap, Marius." Karen replied, "It would probably be an intelligent idea if we didn't move, at least until we figure this out." Said Marius. Before Marius could say another word, the ground beneath him began to quake. The ground separated eight feet in width, rocks crumbled as they fell beneath. Karen slowly stepped away from the trap, she mistakenly set off, and she peered down into the enormous gap in the ground. Eyes glimmered back up as she transformed into her white wolf form, she yelled, as she tossed Marius back to safety and then herself. "Marius, go find Regis!" Karen said.

Marius stood petrified as if his feet have lost all recollections on how to move. Two red paws clutched the edge of where the ground had separated, and the beast had begun to pull itself up. "A red wolf, my god I've never seen one in person. They've been rumored to be extinct." Said Karen. Red wolves were amongst the most gruesome beasts known by all the purebred species. A freak of nature amongst freaks of nature purely bred by evil; forged in flames. Apart from white wolves, red wolves are one of the most deadly of their kind. Karen still in front of Marius springs into the air colliding with the beast. Marius takes off and begins to make his way toward the last two huts. Marius's feat would prove to be an arduous one since both huts lay in the rear region of the mountain on opposite sides. Marius arrives at the first hut and notices the first one was well protected by steel thorns intertwined from every angle like vines. "That's an interesting way to keep unwanted guests out," I said. My eyes still pitch black, skin cold and stiff as granite in the winter time had appeared from nowhere. Blood splattered on my clothing and face, and I stood there with a dark grin. Despite the mayhem transpiring I still appeared flawless and unaffected by it all. The perfect killer, even in all the stench you could still be drawn in by his scent. Regardless of the dozens of main arteries my teeth had broken into as I freed my victims of life, I remained intact. "I assume you've come to assist me with this task Mason?" Marius asked. "I have, how harmful do you gather this hut's defenses are to me?" I replied, "Oh, no more than a mosquito bite would be to me." Marius replied. Without any thought; I advance towards the hut. Simultaneously the vines like steel thorns come alive. Limb by limb they latch onto me. The door springs open and the vines launch me inside of the hut. Still attached to my arm, they begin to saw into my granite-like skin. Almost effortlessly I free myself of the vines one by one. "I applaud your strength Mr. Shrinewald; your gifts seem to be unparalleled." Says Lady Phalanx "You've gone through all this trouble to get me here Phalanx when you learn that I won't yield to you?!" I said. "I never expected that you would crumble under the multiple pressures I've applied to you, however; I did anticipate you not being alone in your adventure. If I cannot draw your blood from you volun-tarily, I will provide incentives for you to do so yourself!" Said Lady Phalanx "What have you done?!" I asked "I have provided you with the incentive that would require you to give me what my clan and I have longed for over a century. We long for perfection, and it's a curse to be a prime and not to possess any of the gifts given to primes by the elements; gifts a prime should be born with!" Said Lady Phalanx "The elements have a peculiar way of rounding things off, don't they Sara?" I replied.

"You don't have the issues of having to discover new ways to survive, and the Phalanx Clan were awarded the short end of the stick from the very beginning. You Shrinewalds have always tried to deny your destiny, what a waste of power. You deny your heritage, so I'll drain your legacy from your veins and create a new one!" Said Lady Phalanx "Since it's my legacy within my veins you long so desperately for, you will know the wrath of contesting a Shrinewald as well!" I said. My teeth lengthen as my hand darts out and grip Lady Phalanx's neck. Back and forth we struggle to sink our teeth into one another neck. Lady Phalanx draws back to gather herself; immovable I remain in place. On my fingertips, I have traces of Lady Phalanx's blood. "So the strumpet bitch does bleed," I said licking her blood from my fingers. In a rage and feeling feeble Lady Phalanx attacks me once more, spinning around from behind she pulls my head back towards her teeth. "I will fulfill my destiny!" Screams Lady Phalanx "Oh no, not today!" I replied. I toss her over my shoulder onto the floor, with my knee to her throat I draw my hand back to end the fiery quarrel. Lady Phalanx screams as she breaks free of my restraint and scampers away in a flash. "I will fulfill my destiny, Mason! Your blood will be mine!" Lady Phalanx screams as she runs away.

SEPARATION FOR THE HUNT

I open the hut door and gaze across the mountain region scanning for any more potential threats. "See anything?" Asks Karen. "No, just this funny-looking guy we've been fighting tooth and nail over." I replied. "Regis!?" Karen asks excited "Yes Regis, Marius is walking back with him now." I replied. Marius is met halfway by Karen and myself; excited to see our long-lost friend we greet him with a hug. "Hey wise guy, next time you decide to come up missing, don't." I said. "I'll keep that in mind." Regis says smiling "By the way you look like," "Don't remind me, Mason." Regis says interrupting me. "It's finally over." Karen says gleefully

"No, it's just beginning; I have to leave Baton Rouge for a while." I replied. "How long will you be gone?" Karen asked, "At least until I can resolve this bounty issue." I said. "So you're going to run, what about school?" Karen asked. "Where ever my friends or my clan is I cannot be. It won't be safe, you see what we just had to go through to get Regis back, and they were unprepared. The next time they come after me, it will only be worse. I need to learn how to thoroughly use my gifts so that I can protect the folks I care about." I said. "I understand." Said Karen, looking down at the ground "Hey, none of that, I'm coming back for you; I promise." I said, "I know, it's just that things won't be the same." Karen replied, "Aww, I'll believe you'll manage just fine; after all you still have Regis." I said. "Yeah, sometimes speaking to Regis is like speaking to a rock." Said Karen. "Hey, I heard that! Look, Mason, Karen and Marius; I'm really grateful for what you guys did. Thank you for that." Said Regis "What are friends for?" I replied, "Mason, we really must be going; you are still a wanted man." Said Marius. "Right, Nebulous will be here shortly to take you back to the campus." I said staring at Karen. "You gotta go, you look out for yourself." Said Karen. "Oh, I'll be a click away; in the shadows watching you from afar, so you watch yourself." I replied, "I'm a big girl; I can take care of myself." Karen said, "Don't I know it." I said. "Yeah besides, she has me; her dependable ally. We'll be ok, where'd they go?" Said Regis. Within an instant, Mason and Marius had vanished into the smoke. I learned many things during my first year at Luce, made invaluable friends and gained timeless enemies. Marius knew that I would have to separate myself to begin my trek to become the hybrid I was destined to be. Sure I had unlocked my natural born killer side, but I also unlocked parts of me that made me overflow with affection for the ones I loved.

Mason was our friend; we knew one day we'd see him again. We also knew that his enemies were now our enemies. They would attempt to use us in ways to get to him. Two months flew by, and I woke up and followed through with my daily routine before class. A Troverter stood outside Lunar Hall waiting for me to head out to class. "Hello, to what pleasure do I owe this visit to?" Karen asked sarcastically. "Lady Phalanx would like to see you." Said the Troverter. "Unlike you and her buddy, I have a class to attend, and she can wait." Said Karen. "SHE WILL SEE YOU NOW!" Said the Troverter in a firm burly voice. Not intending to make a scene Karen decided to go willingly. Karen thought with all the pressure on Regis and her; they couldn't afford any more massacres. Karen figured if things took a plunge for the worse she would turn and maul her way out. When Karen arrived at Lady Phalanx's office, they directed her towards the basement. The basement was dark, wet, and molding; however, a trace of silver lingered in the air forcing its way out the vents. Chains were bolted to the walls; there were rooms with bars and some with doors with no windows. Karen tuned in on the constant drip of water coming from what appeared to be a large faucet. The Troverters took her to the very last room at the end of the hall. The room had a silver-like ceiling with padded walls that appeared to be soundproof.

There the battered and newly scarred broken Lady Phalanx stood. "Ms. Cartwright, so nice to see you looking a bit, somber." Said Lady Phalanx "You look a bit humbled I might add, wouldn't have anything to do with a certain Shrinewald would it?!" Karen said facetiously. "Oh, my run in is but the brim of what you will encompass Ms. Cartwright." Lady Phalanx replied, "Nice sadistic room, are you going to torture me?" Karen asked still humorous "Of course not, that would be too kind; chain her up." Lady Phalanx ordered. Unable to transform into her white wolf being due to the silver-lined room designed to interrogate and contain wolves Karen remained in human form. "What's this about?!" Asked Karen. "You know, when I was your age, I would sneak off to witness the detox process of blood luster's in this very basement. This basement back then was not only used to contain and detox blood luster's but voices who were possessed by vile apparitions and oh my favorite, unruly werewolves; especially white ones. You're probably wondering why you can't turn as well I'm assuming? Well since you'll be my guest for a very long time, I'll let you in on a little secret. That metal you smell circulating through the vents: it's not silver; it's white gold and maliciously deadly to white wolves. It breaks the werewolf's anatomy down from the inside out. It also makes you insanely hungry. It will take quite a bit of time to break you. Seeing as time is on our side, we will prevail." Said Lady Phalanx "I don't know anything, you're wasting your time; and even if I did, I'd never tell you!" Karen says laughing as she spits in Phalanx's face. "Oh, I figured your fidelity to Mason would be an issue. Luckily for me, I've developed an incentive for you, just in case you decide to change your mind." Lady Phalanx replied wiping her face "What are you up to, why, why are you doing this?!" Karen asked, "Just tell me what I want to know, and you may run off freely to class." Said Lady Phalanx. Above Karen there lay a large water tank laced in white gold; this would be a slow torture method and Lady Phalanx's first effort to probe Karen for any information on Mason's whereabouts. "I don't know where he is, where ever he is, once he returns; you'll pay dearly for this!" Karen threatened. "Oh, I do look forward to our little party! By the way, once your immune system breaks down, your skin will begin to deteriorate; then you'll need to feed. You will not be rational; you'll be so animal-istic, raging hunger will blind you! I have provided you with a sample of the only blood you'll smell for the dura-tion of your stay here; is it coming together? Yes, yes, your precious friend's blood, Regis Knight's!" Lady Phalanx said, "YOU BITCH, I'LL KILL YOU!" Karen screamed "No my sweet, but when the time is right, you will kill your friend if you don't tell me what I want to know!" Said Phalanx with a sinister grin "NOOOOO!" Screamed Karen. "The choice is yours, Cartwright... Ciao!" Said Lady Phalanx.

www.ingramcontent.com/pod-product-compliance
Lightning Source LLC
Chambersburg PA
CBHW071130250626

47159CB00006B/2188